THE CHAMELEON EFFECT

JOE ARDEN

This is a work of fiction. Names, characters, places, brands, media, and incidents are either the products of the author's imagination or are used fictitiously. The author acknowledges the trademarked status and trademark owners of various products referenced in this work of fiction, which have been used without permission. The publication/use of these trademarks is not authorized, associated with, or sponsored by the trademark owners.

Rebecca Hodgkins, Editor
Cover Design by Emily Wittig
Adam Perry, Cover Model
Chris Carroll, Cover Model Photographer
Champagne Book Design, Interior Book Design

To my mother.

Always.

THE CHAMELEON EFFECT PLAYLIST

Fitter Happier, Radiohead

Come Undone, Duran Duran

Undone - The Sweater Song, Weezer

Going to California, Led Zeppelin

The Waiting, Tom Petty

Midnight In A Perfect World, DJ Shadow

Blackbird, The Beatles

40 Oz. To Freedom, Sublime

You Know I'm No Good, Amy Winehouse

One, Harry Nilsson

Crash Into Me, Dave Matthews Band

Que Sera, Wax Tailor

Tear in my Heart, Twenty One Pilots

Let Me Back In, Rilo Kiley

Glory Box (live), Portishead

Tiny Dancer, Elton John

Love and Happiness, Al Green

THE CHAMELEON EFFECT

PROLOGUE

MOST PEOPLE THINK LA IS THIS FAKE, PLASTIC TOWN. BUT I DON'T. I think it's one of the most honest places in the world. I mean, are Los Angelinos superficial and fixated on body image? Yeah. Do they spend all day long obsessing over calories and workout trends? Sure. Are there more juice bars than McDonald's in this town? Probably, I don't know. I haven't counted. But you know what? The people here—they're upfront about it. Everyone may be trying to look like something they're not, to be someone they're not: fitter, happier, more productive... But no one pretends that's NOT what's going on. Los Angeles is a city of dreamers. No one here, no matter how old, has given up. Everyone here still believes in something. Some of them still believe in everything.

Plenty of people think it's a cliché that every barista has a screenplay. They find it ridiculous that every bouncer hopes to be the next Vin Diesel. I think it's beautiful. A city full of unapologetic storytellers. The place where people come to fearlessly invent fantastical worlds. Aspirers ceaselessly creating brave heroes and happy endings. Not because they aren't aware of all the ugly life can throw at a person, but rather because they choose to be positive in the face of it all.

Plus, the food here is really good. But I digress.

Why am I talking about all this? Because I'm one of those dreamers, one of this city's storytellers. But in the process of dreaming my dreams and living my story, I got lost in the clouds. I was spinning enough yarn to keep me warm all winter, but then I met her, and everything changed. One plunge into her soft brown eyes; one knee-wobbling smile from her full lips; one innocent conversation and my dreams were re-written. Instantly.

Meeting her felt like one strong tug on my heart, and just like that first pulled thread on an old sweater, I began to come undone.

HOLLYWOOD

CHAPTER ONE

"WHENEVER YOU'RE READY, MR. O'CONNELL," THE CASTING director drones from behind the cold stare of the camera lens. I take a deep breath as I assess the couch full of poker faces staring back at me, focus my attention on the red record light just to the left of the camera lens, picture a real person staring back, and start the scene. This is my third callback for a TV guest star in as many weeks. Another chance for that big break. One step away from turning the title of 'aspiring actor' into the elusive one of 'working actor'.

"I thought I told you not to come around here anymore." I dive into the opening beat of the scene, lines memorized, confidence high.

"I've tried to get over you, Johnny, but you're under my skin," The casting assistant drones from a chair off to the side. His flat delivery is only slightly more distracting than his low baritone.

"I don't know how many times I have to tell you, Isabella, we're through."

"But Johnny, I need you and I know you still need me," he continues in his monotone.

I remain focused on that blinking red dot and fire my final line to the room. "If I still needed you, then I wouldn't have gotten rid of *this*." In a controlled but fierce movement, I pull at my sleeve cuff to reveal an arm that has never had a tattoo on it, but for the purposes of this scene, an arm that *used* to have a tattoo on it.

I hold my final beat, then break character on an exhale and look over at the couch.

"Thank you, Mr. O'Connell," the casting director lies. "We'll be in touch."

And now for the acting no one tells you about, the scene work they don't have a class for: making a bold exit. I plaster a smile on my face, wave at the sea of disinterested faces, and head out of the room.

I walk through the lobby sprinkled with bros in waffle Henleys and designer jeans: the competition. A sparsely decorated waiting area of fit young guys all mumbling to themselves, the scents of Acqua di Gio and Axe clashing in the air, like a psych ward inside an Abercrombie and Fitch. We don't all look identical, but we definitely all have a few things in common: flat stomachs, broad shoulders, and jawlines that could cut glass. My shaggy, light-brown hair screams LA surf bum, but the flecks of red in my neatly trimmed beard help set me apart. And sure, at twenty-six, I might be a few years older than some of these guys, but my looks haven't lost a step.

That's not me being cocky, that's an objective evaluation of my physical presence, a critical part of any actor's journey. Know your type. *How can you find the right roles for you if you don't know how other people see you?* At least that's what my personal trainer/fellow aspiring actor/best friend Devontay says. Or what our acting teacher told us. Or something I read on a billboard somewhere. Anyway, it's good advice and I do my best to follow it. Be self-aware.

Right now, that awareness is telling me that I probably punted another callback and since this audition brought me over the hill and all the way down to Mid-Wilshire, the best course of action is to pop in on the older bro. Nothing helps hit the reset button like a little family time. The lap pool and hot tub don't hurt either.

I pop off a quick text to him before hopping into my burnt sienna '86 Volvo, banging a left on Pico, and cruising into Beverly Hills.

CHAPTER TWO

One can estimate the overall value of a home in Beverly Hills by the size of its hedges. The richer people are, the more they like to hide it all behind big green shrubbery. My brother likes to buck this trend. He's got a beautiful spread on a shady, tree-lined street but he likes fostering a sense of community. To invite that neighborly spirit, his bright, open thirty-five hundred square foot contemporary home sits behind a tasteful, red archway door and neatly trimmed boxwoods that reach only shoulder height. What can I say? My brother is a man of the people.

I punch in the code next to the door, and as I step through the entryway, I am bombarded by a blur of pink fluff. My six-year-old niece has rattled off three sentences before I've even had a chance to catch my breath from the force of her enthusiastic slam into my stomach.

"...And then Abigail said *Madeleine* was the coolest girl book character, but then Stacy said *Eloise* before Tasha said *Ladybug Girl,* and before I could answer, the bell rang and we had to go back inside and I never got to tell them and I think my answer is Rapunzel, but I also love Olive from the

Hoot and Olive books, and now I don't even know who's right. What do you think Uncle Will?"

I pause briefly just to make sure Lexi is finished, then fill in the silence. "I'm sure if all those girls met up in one story, they'd kick some serious butt."

"Whoa, I never even thought of that. I'm gonna go draw that like right this second," Lexi beams as she bounds back into the house, sidestepping her dad on the way in.

My brother stands outside his place, one hand on the front door, the other ushering me up the walkway.

"Long time no see, little bro. To what do we owe the midweek visit?"

"Oh, you know, just swung by Cartier to grab that new watch Bieber was flossing on Insta, figured I'd pop in and say what's up," I say in my best impression of whoever the hell that guy would be.

Ryan laughs and side-hugs me as we walk in together. "Come out back. Your bathing suit's in the cabana, iced tea's in the pitcher, and Hazel's grilling turkey burgers. You're staying for dinner." It isn't a question, and damn it feels good to be with them. Nothing soothes the sting of professional defeat quite like an afternoon with the family.

Two hours and one relaxing swim later, the four of us are sitting in the backyard polishing off a mean side of honeyed Brussels sprouts that Hazel made to go with that killer turkey burger.

"I must say, William, I'm terribly sorry to hear that you don't feel this one went your way. We saw you last month in that play and you were clearly the standout," my extremely posh, extremely British, extremely talented sister-in-law Hazel consoles. She and my brother met ten years ago while he was studying abroad. She had just finished fashion school and had dreamt of seeing the States. They came back together and haven't separated since. Now he's on the fast track with one of the elite real estate companies in the city and Hazel turned her love of fashion and design into a boutique interior decorating business. Or really, I should say more like an enterprise. She's got more clients than she knows what to do with, a second business staging houses for Ryan's company, and her own line of pillows at West Elm. I didn't even realize people actually designed pillows.

"Not sure my acting is as good as these Brussels, Haze. What did you do to these?" I compliment her sincerely, but I'm also trying to deflect my own frustrations.

"A hint of sriracha is the—" but before Hazel can finish, she's cut off by a determined Lexi. "That's ridiculous, Uncle Will. Remember that show that Mom and Dad took me to? You were the most awesomest thing in it. Everyone was laughing and you did all those cool voices. Brussel sprouts are icky, you are not."

"Why, thank you, milady," I respond, invoking a highbrow English accent to reprise my role of the prince on the patio. "'Tis a fair thing to receive this wonderful praise from a lady of such distinction."

Ryan laughs softly from his spot at the table, plate wiped clean. "Not gonna lie, bro. You are good at that. The way you just turn it on and off like that. It's impressive."

"In Russia, we are not allowed to receive compliments," I say in a throaty Eastern European twang. "And in France, it is considered rude to be nice to people." This in a thick French drawl.

The family laughs as Hazel says, "You're a chameleon, Will."

"Well thanks, but so far, it's just a neat party trick. Not putting any gas in the old Volvo, if you know what I mean."

"Keep at it, bro," Ryan tells me as Hazel adds, "Your break will come."

I think back on the last eight years of my life. If I had gone into medicine, I'd be a doctor by now. Instead, I'm living in a studio apartment in Venice, because let's get serious, why move to Los Angeles if you're not going to be near the water? Right now, I'm spending more time bartending than I am acting, but it's not for lack of effort. Acting classes, scene study, improv. I am putting in the work and I know that I've got to keep at it. Confidence is such a critical tool in this industry, but it's hard to keep believing in yourself when no one's taken notice in almost a decade.

Still deep in my own thoughts, I blurt out, "it's just so frustrating. I feel like so many British and Australian actors get cast in all these American roles because they have this accent they can switch on and off."

"Well," my brother counters. "To be fair, most of them are working because they're really damn good."

"Yeah, but it's not a two-way street. Any time there's a casting breakdown for a British character, it always says 'authentic accents only'. I'm not saying Jude Law's not talented, I'm just saying let me have a crack at a gritty Londoner trying to turn his MMA career around after a bad accident."

"Well, that was oddly specific, but I hear what you're saying, bro." My brother replies sympathetically.

"Or, if authenticity is the name of the game, then it's gotta work both ways. Brits play Brits and Americans play Americans. I'm not asking for a leg up; I'm just looking for parity."

I sigh as I sip my iced tea, watching the fading light dance off the glistening blue water of the pool. Another perfect LA sunset and I am not feeling it.

Just then, Hazel's face lights up. "You should do that."

"Do what?"

"The accent thing."

"What are you talking about?"

She sits up in her lounger, eyes dancing mischievously. "Pretend to be Irish. You're good with accents, yeah?"

"My acting teacher Lenny Schneider says I'm one of the best he's ever heard."

"Well, for four hundred dollars a month, I'm sure he's happy to dole out the compliments." My brother needles in, but Hazel is on a roll now and ignores him.

She's shifted so near to the edge of her chair, she almost tips it over as words pour from her mouth. "That's beside the point. Focus. You just said a ton of work is going to overseas actors. So, you pretend to be from Great Britain or Ireland—"

"Those are two different places. Did you know that?" I whisper aside to my brother.

"I did know that," he whispers back with a roll of his eyes.

Hazel ignores us, continuing on. "So, you say you're from Dublin or wherever and maybe it helps you tip the scales? Doctor your resume a little. Add a college and a couple theaters no one's ever heard of. Walk in with a brogue, switch on a dime, and blow them away." She sits up straight, arms spread in offering.

"That's insane. Totally ridiculous. If I got caught, I'd never work in this town again."

"So, basically, your life now." My brother, again.

"Ouch, man."

"Sorry, but you know..."

"Yeah, no. I get it. Point taken."

I take a long pull from my glass.

"Maybe this iced tea is starting to get to me, but Hazel, dude... this isn't the worst idea I've ever heard."

"No, it's the best you've ever heard. What do you have to lose?"

It's a fair question. I've been working hard at this for a long time. Everyone's always talking about their angle, what they have to do to get their foot in the door, hell, maybe one day this will make a great story on The Late Show. Yeah, this could be... But before I can get myself fully psyched up, the wise words of a young babe bring me crashing back to earth.

"But wait, Uncle W. Haven't you been seen around town? Like, don't people know your name from auditionings and stuff?"

"Um, that's a really good point, Lex. Not sure why we didn't think of that."

"That's fine," Hazel thinks out loud. "If we're already doctoring your resume, no reason we can't tweak the name a bit too."

"Sure," my brother adds. "Celebrities use fake names all the time."

"I like my name though."

"So, don't change the whole thing," Hazel suggests. "Doesn't get much more Irish than O'Connell, so let's come up with a new first name."

"What about Michael?" I throw out to get the ball rolling.

"Sounds a bit like an old priest." Hazel immediately shuts that down.

"Connor?" My brother offers, getting in the mix.

"Too many 'Kuh' sounds," Lexi supplies. "I like Will."

"I do too, Lil Sprite, but it's too much like my full name," I tell her with a smile.

"But this isn't," Hazel starts with a Cheshire Cat grin, leaving her next thought hanging in the air before actually speaking. "What about...Liam." She pauses again with an arch of her eyebrow. "Liam O'Connell."

"Liam O'Connell," I say, trying the name out in my mouth, and I gotta say, it sounds like a name that belongs in lights. "I like it." But that momentary enthusiasm quickly gives way to doubt. "But I'm not sure I can pull this off."

My brother attempts encouragement. "Hey, don't they say you're nobody until you're somebody in this town, anyway. No one will even remember the old you."

"Well, that's not as reassuring as you might have thought. But I hear what you're saying." I mull this all over before continuing, "I do have an audition coming up this Friday. For a casting director I've never seen before."

"Perfect," Hazel says, beaming.

"You ready for your closeup, Mr. Liam O'Connell?" My brother asks confidently.

I look him dead in the eye, and fearlessly and recklessly tell him, "Feck it."

"Language, Uncle W!" Lexi shouts.

"Shit, sorry, Lex," I stumble, totally losing my accent. "And yep. I heard that. Did it again. Sorry."

"Oh yeah," my brother adds sarcastically, "this is gonna go great."

CHAPTER THREE

TWO DAYS LATER I FIND MYSELF STARING BACK AT THIS NEW ME ON my phone, checking my hair and collar before they call my name. Or my new name, anyway. Or part of my name, I guess.

Doctored resume in hand? Check.

Back story committed to memory? Check.

Total disregard for the rules of civil society and a reckless desire to destroy my life? That would be a final check from me, the man just stupid enough to think this might actually work.

"Liam O'Connell?" The receptionist intones over her clipboard.

"Ta, dat's me," I respond, perhaps laying it on a little thick.

"You're up," she says without even so much as glancing up at me. Ok, that's a good start, I suppose. No response is what I'm looking for. Blending in, that's the name of the game.

I take one deep breath, then march through the doors to meet my fate. The faces on the couch are different from previous auditions, but still somehow the same. Lifeless, expressionless, disinterested.

I eye the red tape on the floor and walk over to it, dropping my headshot and resume off on the coffee table as I do. I plant my feet and stare at the opposite wall. This is it. Once I open my mouth, there's no going back. Eight years and no one's taken an interest in Will—time to give Liam a crack.

"Cheers everyone. I'm Liam. Pleasure to be here. Real excited to dive in," I rattle off in a brisk Dublin accent. "Now, quick question before I get started. I assume you'd like this detective read in the same accent I did for the first audition, right?"

"Um, yes. Mr. O'Connell. The character is from Chicago. Recently moved to Idaho to expand his territory, so standard Midwest American if that's not a problem."

"No problem at all," I say, more truthfully than he knows. I shake that thought and look directly at the cameraman who points and states, "We're rolling. Whenever you're ready."

I find that blinking red light next to the lens, bore my soul straight into it, and snap back to my normal voice. "Now you listen to me, Marcus. We have the drugs. We've tested them. And you and your boys stomped all over my product. What I offer is pure. My reputation is built on quality and trust. And you degraded my quality, so I don't trust you..."

"Man, I already told that other guy, I don't know anything I ain't already said." The reader cues me for my final line. "We paid you in full. That was the agreement."

"The arrangement was you sell the product I supply. Not cut it up with a bunch of baby laxatives and pocket the difference. Yeah? Now, the question is... what I am gonna do with you," I finish with some gravel in my voice. I hold my eyeline on the camera light for one more beat, then relax and look over to the couch.

And holy shit, those cold, lifeless eyes are...what is that expression? Interest? Confusion? Oh God, are they on to me already? This was a terrible idea. Why would I listen to my brother and his ridiculous wife? They're rich. Nothing bad ever happens to them.

Before I can run from the room, a guy in a flannel button-down leans over from the couch and eyes my resume. The silence is probably only a couple seconds, but it feels like I'm standing there for the duration of a Phish song. In concert.

My past and future flash before my eyes somehow simultaneously. Growing up in Cincinnati watching every Edward Norton and Michelle Williams film I can get my hands on. Performing Jimmy Stewart monologues for Grandpa at Thanksgiving. Reading *Variety* and *Entertainment Weekly* that I snuck inside my textbooks. And in an instant, I'm back there. A laughingstock. The boy who thought he could fool Hollywood. Now the only costume he wears is his Skyline Chili uniform. *You want to make that bowl a three-way for just a dollar more, sir?*

Back in the room, the man holding my resume breaks my reverie. "Looks like you've done most of your training in Ireland. How long you been over here, Liam?"

"Yeah, I finished up a run as Stanley in *Streetcar* at the Gaiety in Dublin, and figured it was high time I gave the States a crack. Been at it almost a year now. I love doing theatre, but my heart's always belonged to film." I pronounce that last word with the two syllables the Irish give it for no reason I can understand.

And no, in case you're wondering, I haven't played Stanley before, but hey, if you're gonna give yourself a made-up past, might as well make it a good one. You should have seen my *Hamlet* in Limerick.

He looks up and down the couch in a series of silent exchanges with the other members of the creative team, then looks back at me. "Darlene will give you a call in an hour to schedule a fitting for tomorrow and we film this on the lot on Monday."

"I'm sorry," I respond, so shocked I almost lose the accent, but pull it back in time. "Are you saying I've got the part? Like, right now?"

"That's right, Drug Lord. You're hired. I'll see you on set, Monday."

I float out of the room on a cloud of smiles and thank-yous. I didn't think people got hired on the spot like that. Of course, what did I know? I've never been hired before at all. As I get to my car and that initial rush of adrenaline begins to dissipate, a new thought comes crashing into my head: what the hell have I gotten myself into?

CHAPTER FOUR

"SO LET ME GET THIS STRAIGHT," MY BEST FRIEND AND PERSONAL trainer, Devontay, starts in as he hits his stopwatch. I jump into plank pose and hold. We're in one of his favorite spots for outdoor workouts—a little patch of grass on Ocean Avenue. Runners and cyclists on one side of us, the Pacific Ocean below us on the other. While I'm on my elbows focusing on my breathing, sun warming my bare back, Von continues rehashing everything I told him during the kettlebell session that preceded this ab workout.

"You went to an audition—" He begins, pacing in a circle around me, his sleeveless weightlifting tee exposing his giant shoulders and biceps.

"Callback," I correct him.

"I'm sorry, right. A callback for a scene in a network TV show with a fake resume—"

I interrupt again, a little out of breath. "Doctored. I mean, most of the info on there was accurate, just upsold a bit."

"Ok, sure. It's your resume, but like, with some grilled shrimp on top.

So, you give them a doctored resume, introduce yourself as Liam, with an apparently passable Irish accent—"

"No one called me out."

"—Then slipped into your *normal* voice to read the copy, and they booked you. On the spot?"

"That's the long and the short of it," I huff out as my abs begin to sing in pain.

"And now you have a costume fitting in an hour for this role you booked on the basis of this lie. Where you will now, presumably, have to keep up this ruse the entire time."

"Speaking of time, where are we on this set?" I ask, feeling my knees begin to quiver.

He glances at the stopwatch with barely a look. "Yeah, it's ten seconds past, but what does time even mean anymore in this alternate reality you've created, Will?"

I immediately drop out of plank and arch up into cobra pose to relieve some of the pressure on my midsection. I love the cut of my abs and the way I feel in a pair of well-worn jeans, but damn do I not like the work required to maintain it. The stand-up paddleboarding helps, but it's Devontay who gets them chiseled. He's the Michelangelo of the midsection. He stands over me now, blocking out that unforgiving SoCal sun, making the Santa Monica wind feel just a tad chillier.

"You didn't think this through, Will. I get you're hungry for success and no one deserves a break more than you, but is this really how you want to go about it? By pretending to be something you're not?"

Devontay always gives it to me straight. He and I met my first month in LA and have been tight ever since. We ran into each other at one of those free workout stations that a lot of LA parks provide, then saw each other again that night at an improv class we'd both signed up for. We didn't need much more convincing than that. Working out and working on our craft have been our shared dreams ever since. And taking road trips, and drinking beers, and a bunch of other stuff, but we keep each other focused on those main goals the whole time.

Von's also been studying martial arts and looking into stunt doubling and motion capture work. The way he's toned his body, he could fill in for a video game sports star or Hollywood supervillain any day. Right now, he's eyeing me down like Drago glaring daggers at Rocky.

I sit up on my knees to answer him. "I've got a firm backstory. I thought through the ins and outs of this, and dude, the proof is in the smoothie. After eight years of being overlooked, I booked the first spot I read for. Or Liam did, I should say."

"No, you should not. *Will.*" He manages a firm reprimand simply by saying my name. "Just go to the fitting now. Then find the director on Monday and come clean. He'll understand. You'll nail the scene, and you can build your real reputation on the back of your real identity. The one you've been working so hard to create for this long." Von has crouched down beside me during this speech, and it's another reminder of what a great friend he is. Caring and thoughtful.

"I'll think about it," I tell him, meaning it. "Right now, I've gotta get home and shower before this fitting." I stand up and grab my water bottle and keys. "Oh," I say, glancing back at Von. "In the meantime, you should probably start calling me Liam. Just in case."

He stares straight through me. "Well, Dr. Jekyll, it seems you've created yourself a Mister and, if you don't figure this out soon, he's going to have no place to Hyde."

CHAPTER FIVE

Charming—if slightly forced—literary puns aside, Von had a point. How much of myself am I willing to sacrifice in pursuit of this goal? Am I being disingenuous? Dishonest? And just practically speaking, how long can I actually keep this charade up? These thoughts pour through my mind while water cascades down my sandy brown hair. The warmth drapes across my aching shoulders and pecs, releasing some of the tension starting to build up. Devontay's burnout kettlebell session might have something to do with it too, but hey, the toned ridges of my neck and upper back along with the sinewy curves of my biceps speak for themselves, so bring on the steamy relief.

Towel dried, soft gray tee and jeans thrown on, then out the door for this fitting. Rita gets me there with ten minutes to spare, so I park and spend a few mindless minutes on TikTok before heading in. Rita, you ask. That's the name of my rust-red mid-80s Volvo with original beige leather interior. My dad insisted my entire life that every car be given a woman's name. "Treat her with respect and the right combination of patience and control, and she'll be good to you for a long time. Same applies in life." Not sure what my father's stance on same-sex driving is, but some traditions never die.

Anyway, when I moved to LA and bought this Swedish tank with just over a hundred thousand miles on her, I figured naming her after one of the most famous redheads in American cinema was appropriate. The sobriquet reminds me of Saturdays in the garage with Dad, even if I did end up getting most of my relationship advice from my mother.

As I enter the office building, I double-check my notes to make sure I'm in the right place. Confirming the suite number on the directory, I slide into the elevator and head up to the third floor. Since my fitting is on the weekend, they've sent me to the costume shop's office and workspace rather than on set. May not be a trailer on the Warner lot, but I am pretty amped regardless. My first professional costume fitting.

Before I open the door, I take one steadying breath. Time to turn off Will and turn on Liam. Though the person's the same, the voice most definitely is not, so I've got to take a moment to get into character. Slightly under my breath, I mumble a sentence that helps anchor me in the accent. "Dis is me life and it's the right time to shine."

I open the door to a sea of color and fabric. Two giant workstations fill most of the room with scissors, swatches, and sketches, taking up every inch of available counter space. Two women whose faces I can't see are hunched over sewing machines, feeding fabric through.

"Welcome, come in, take your shoes off and wait over there," a woman with red-rimmed glasses and a head full of curls directs me while eyeing two pairs of pants on the table in front of her. "This one," she says to no one in particular, then picks up that pair and drapes them next to one of the sewing machines in use. "Label these as Jake's for the apartment scene in episode four."

With that, she has floated my way and somehow seems to be moving without taking actual steps or actual breaths. She continues talking. "My name is Carlotta Garcia. I am the Costume Designer for *Boise Patrol.* You must be Liam, playing Drug Thug Rogers." She rattles this off in her lilting

Latina accent, grabs a clipboard seemingly from thin air, reviews it, and peers over her glasses at me.

"Typecasting, am I right?" I offer with a big smile, but Ms. Garcia is all business. She powers on.

"Raven will take your measurements, then we will see if we have any looks here for you to try on. Bueno?"

"Uh, yeah, that's grand." I stumble as she sets the clipboard down and floats back over to a pile of fabric.

My attention shifts to a thick head of hair held in place precariously by two chopsticks behind one of the sewing machines. Her head rises, and holy shit, like Aphrodite rising from that clamshell, she becomes more stunning as she stands. Or was it an oyster shell? Or a mussel? Doesn't fucking matter because I'm transfixed by something far more beautiful.

That bun of black hair opens up to a porcelain face and toffee-colored eyes that stick me right in place. The creamy paleness of her skin is set off even more by her jet-black hair. I take in the gentle swell of her breasts under her artfully torn Metallica tee. The shirt falls loosely over her, but there's no hiding the dips and curves underneath. And though her top has short sleeves, her arms aren't bare. Strokes of black and red ink paint her skin. Curves and lines; stories and dreams dance on her flesh.

Before I know it, she's right in front of me, clipboard in hand, measuring tape draped over her shoulders.

"Hi, I'm Raven." She pulls a pencil from behind one ear, almost as if by magic, or perhaps I've become so hypnotized by her that I just hadn't noticed it there. And words fall from my mouth as if in a trance, a hypnotic remembering of phrases I memorized years ago.

"Deep into that darkness peering, long I stood there wondering, fearing. Doubting, dreaming dreams no mortal ever dared to dream before…" I half chant, half mumble.

Her eyes ignite as she looks up. "That's the first time someone hasn't just said 'Nevermore.'"

"Philistines, the lot of them. I'm Wi—uh, Liam. Liam O'Connell." *Fuck.* Pull it together, man. "Sorry, I'm rambling a bit. This is my first TV role, so

I'm a might nervous," I say in an attempt to cover the stumble I had over my name.

A hint of a grin parts her ruby-red lips. "You've already got the job. Nothing to be nervous about now," she offers in a lyrical voice with just a hint of rasp, like Amy Winehouse. I would gladly hand this woman my Stella and fly.

"Yep, cheers. Thanks. So, what do you need from me?" I ask, steering my mind back to work.

"I'll start at the top and work my way down. All I need from you is to relax," she says as she wraps the tape around my neck and begins making notes on her pad. I stop myself from saying I'd like to do the same thing to her, but I can't stop myself from thinking it. I've only been in this woman's presence for a few short minutes, but she captivates me. I push all those thoughts aside, though, because I am not trying to mix business with pleasure here. Got to keep this super professional. I take a deep breath, relax my knees and let her get to work. The tape measure dances over her fingers and along my body. Neck to shoulder, shoulder to elbow, elbow to wrist, down the length of my arm. Her focus and her calm draw me in.

"You've got this down to a science," I say, commenting on her speed and efficiency.

"Well, I've been doing this for five years now, so it's mostly muscle memory. Take a deep breath in and hold it," she says as she wraps the tape around my chest.

"Pardon me for saying, but you don't look old enough to have been doing anything professional for five years."

"Moved to LA on my nineteenth birthday, started working for Carlotta shortly after that," she says as she jots a few more measurements down on her clipboard.

"Pretty epic birthday present to yourself," I respond casually, thinking about the fact that we have that part of our story in common. But it's not a part of Liam's backstory, so I keep that connection to myself.

"Well, it was time for a change in my life," she says cryptically, "and clothing has always been my passion. So, here I am."

"Brilliant. Well, I'm happy to be in your expert hands," I say with just a hint of flirt behind the words.

The tape measure travels down to my toned stomach and waist, as Raven crouches down to measure my lower half. The view of her looking up at me with those copper eyes has my mind reeling, but between my desire for this job and my need to stay in character, I can't dwell too long on that look, or that feeling in the pit of my stomach it evokes.

Averting my gaze from her eyes only brings it to her arms which are both bare and full of striking ink. I try to focus on her art while she runs the tape measure down my leg, then up my inseam.

"So," I begin, to break the runaway train of thought my mind is racing down, "those are quite a few tattoos. Any special significance to any of them?" Immediately, I realize that might be a little too forward, so I amend, "Sorry. I didn't mean to pry. You obviously don't have to tell me anything you don't want to."

She catches my eye and a smile brushes her lips. The energy between us crackles and it's definitely from more than the intimacy of a costume fitting. A playfulness lights up her face as she says, "Oh, these? Most of them are just notes. I'm awfully forgetful, so I use shorthand on my body. This one is where I left my keys. That butterfly is actually a reminder to unplug my curling iron. It's a whole system."

I laugh. We both laugh. And it feels great. "So, like *Memento.*"

She thinks about this and earnestly replies, "But much lower stakes."

"Yeah, I guess tracking down your wife's murderer is a pretty legit reason to get your body covered in tattoos."

"Whatever gets Guy Pearce to take his shirt off works for me."

We both laugh again, as I make a mental note: *schedule a few extra sessions with Von.*

Carlotta glances our way like a fourth-grade teacher and Raven and I immediately focus back on the work. "Sorry. Don't want to get you in trouble," I whisper conspiratorially, as Raven makes a few more notes on her clipboard.

"You could get me in a lot of trouble with that accent, Mr. O'Connell," Raven purrs *sotto voce* then heads towards Carlotta, but not before locking me in place with a look that lasts just a beat longer than it should, but not nearly as long as I'd like.

Maybe this accent is going to come in handier than I could possibly have imagined, I think to myself as I watch her walk away.

After a quick scan of my measurements, Carlotta floats toward a curtained dressing room pulling shirts and pants from racks along the way. "Liam, step behind here and try some of these combinations on. Though with that body, I'm pretty sure you'll look great in anything we put on you."

I laugh softly at the compliment, then begin trying on outfits. Carlotta barks out her thoughts on each one, Raven takes notes, and I retreat behind the curtain to don the next one. After several rounds of this, Carlotta seems satisfied.

"Perfecto, Liam. We have a few looks that should work. Raven will be there on set Monday to make sure you have everything you need," Carlotta says as I pull my tee over my head and pop back out into the room.

My eyes fixate on that snow-white skin framed by that straight, dark hair. As I leave the office, my mind keeps repeating Carlotta's last words, and I can't help but think how much Raven has everything I need already.

CHAPTER SIX

SUNDAY MORNINGS I GO TO CHURCH. WELL, NOT CHURCH IN THE traditional sense, but my church: the ocean. Up with the sun, I start each Sunday in the water, past the break, stand-up paddleboarding. I love everything about this activity. SUP combines the mental focus of a yoga practice with the physical skills of something you might find on *American Gladiators,* like jousting with the sea.

Once on my feet, the board requires all of my focus, especially in open water. The ocean never rests, she's constantly in motion, she lives and breathes. And as I stand on my board, feet spread, knees bent, and toes rooted firmly to the resin, moving with her rhythms, finding balance by countering her energy, I feel alive. I feel connected. I feel centered.

The ocean and my board keep me honest. A moment of relaxation, a second of lost focus, and boom, my center of gravity is thrown and I'm going for a dip. But if I stay rooted, keep my mind on one thing and one thing only, then all that power, all that oceanic force, becomes controlled and I feel calm.

But it's not long before thoughts of pale skin and piercing eyes race through my mind and I find myself teetering on my board. The cool Pacific snaps my attention back to the present as I plunge in headfirst. Grabbing my paddle, I climb back on and straddle my board. I've got lines to memorize today too, so I decide to head in early to get a jump start on Monday. Probably best to make sure this drug dealer from Boise doesn't get a sunburn anyway.

The rest of my day is spent on my back patio pouring over lines. Once I feel I have a scene memorized, I take a break for a snack or a couple text messages, then go back over what I think I committed to memory, making sure I've got each scene down cold. I firmly believe that acting doesn't begin until the lines become so engrained, they're just like any other kind of muscle memory. In order to be in the moment, to be listening to your scene partner, reacting to each cue, the lines have to be second nature. No pausing, no hesitation, no mental wandering, 'What's my next line? What part of the scene are we on?' The second that happens, I'm out of the moment and the scene falls flat.

By mid-afternoon, I'm feeling pretty strong about the work I've put in, and my phone buzzes with a text from Devontay.

> **Devontay:** Got us on the list for sunset drinks at the Cabana. You down?
>
> **Me:** Not today, my friend. On set tomorrow, so I'm calling it an early night.
>
> **Devontay:** Right. Break a leg, brother. You're gonna crush it.
>
> **Me:** Thanks, man. Nervous, but excited.
>
> **Devontay:** What could go wrong? You've got the luck of the Irish on your side.

He finishes that last text off with a very sarcastic winking emoji and I toss the phone on the table in front of me. I run my lines for tomorrow's scenes just a few more times before I decide I can't possibly know these lines any more than I already do.

I grab a light dinner, a long shower, and a short chill session on the couch with a little TV. I set three alarms to make sure I'm up for my eight a.m. call time, then settle in to bed for the night.

Nerves get the best of me and an hour of restless turning later, I grab my phone to scroll TikTok. Because, you know, nothing calms a person down like twenty-second videos shot directly into your brain rapid-fire.

After a few seconds of scrolling, my thumb freezes as I catch sight of a pair of brown eyes that I would recognize anywhere. The capricious algorithms of fate have led me right to Raven's TikTok…

INTERLUDE #1

Denim to Daaaamn

What up, my Stitches? This your girl Raven and today on Rags to Raven, we are taking our rattiest jeans and turning them into our sexiest shorts. Is there anything worse than shopping for new jeans? Sure, Tinder DMs, but trying on pair after pair of unforgiving pants to find the one that fits, curves, and hugs you just right? It's no fun. That's why once you find a pair of jeans you love, it's easy to forsake all others and become monogamous. But even the most loving relationship needs a little change of pace now and then, so let's take that well-worn pair of denim and turn it into a new pair of Daaaaaaaamn!

All we need are jeans you love, a good pair of scissors, a patch, and an innate belief in the power of change.

First, choose a length you love. The only wrong answer here is the one society dictates. These are *your* shorts. Make them the length *you* want.

Cut, cut, cut. Discard.

Cut, cut, cut. Discard.

Add a piece of personality. If your jeans have a hole, patch it up. Maybe your belt loops need rhinestones. Weave your personality into the fabric…

And voila, your old pair of baby blues just became this summer's new hey-girl-how-are-yous.

CHAPTER SEVEN

NOTHING VALIDATES THE PAST EIGHT YEARS OF HARD WORK LIKE waking up to make it over the hill to the Warner Brothers lot, driving up to the gate, and having my name be on the list. Like a bouncer at Club Dreams-Do-Come-True, the security guard scans my ID, checks it against his clipboard, and lifts the boom arm to let me and rust-red Rita onto the lot. We did it. We made it. We belong.

Well, *Liam* does anyway. But he's still me, right?

I leave that thought unanswered in my head, because frankly, it's already more confusing than I'd thought it would be. After parking the car, I check in with the PA on the lot who sends me to hair and makeup with a couple of script revisions to look over in the meantime. While I'm reviewing a few minor line changes, my sandy brown hair gets some much-needed shaping. She keeps the flowy waves on top but brings the sides in tight. The look says, 'hey, I'm still a little wild, but I've also got enough money to properly take care of my appearance.' I dig it.

Face powdered and a discreet amount of eyeliner applied just under my hazel peepers, a different production assistant takes me to my trailer before meeting with the director. And if I thought being let onto the lot was a dream come true, I was not prepared for the feelings running through me when I saw my name—well part of my name anyway—inside a yellow star taped lovingly to a gray metal trailer door. I take a quick picture of the star and send it off to Devontay and my brother, because I mean, come on! It's my name. On a star. On a film lot. In Hollywood.

A friendly voice pulls me back to the present. "Wardrobe will be by with your rack shortly. And Dennis would love to chat with you before your first scene. I'm Jared. I'll be back to take you to the set in a bit," the guy tells me with a smile and then he presses the headset in his ear and walks off. Dennis Lawson is the director I spoke with at the callback, and I take it as a good sign that everyone on set calls him by his first name.

"Cheers," I reply liltingly, the name on the star a reminder of the persona I must continue to play. Then I bound up the three steps to my room. It's nothing more than a seven-by-five-foot section of a larger trailer that I'm sharing with three other supporting actors on this episode, but the thing that makes this particular space special? It's mine. For the next three days anyway.

I dive into my new, color-coded script to make sure I've got all the changes. Blue pages are unchanged, while yellow pages have received edits. This being my first time on set, I probably wouldn't have known that, but hats off to Lenny Schneider who doesn't just focus on the craft, he makes sure his students are well-versed in the business of the business. "Knowing how to act *on set* is almost as important as knowing how to act *in the scene,*" he's fond of saying. And right now, I'm grateful for his tutelage.

A few minutes later my head is pulled from the script by a rapping at the door. "Hey Liam, you in there?" And I don't need to see the face to know exactly who that throaty voice belongs to. Her timbre burned itself into my memory the second I met her, but only solidified itself after watching that DIY video last night. I rise and go to the door, take one deep breath to remind myself to stay in character, then open the trailer door.

And for the second time in three days, I find myself looking down at an absolute fucking vision. I need another small breath just to recover from what her eyes do to me.

I must have been standing there a little longer than I thought because she's the one to speak again. "Um, I've got a few of your pieces here," Raven says, addressing a clothing rack she's wheeled along beside her.

My brain kicks back into gear, and I thank her as I step down from the trailer to grab the hangers she has for me. "It's grand to see you again," I say before I have a chance to rethink it. It's true, but I probably should have at least started with something to do with the wardrobe for the show.

She smiles but pulls her eyes away from mine. "You too," she almost whispers, and I feel like I can sense a flicker of shared interest, but work is work. It's obviously something that matters to both of us.

"Which look do you want me in first?" I ask, steering us back to calmer waters, confident I'm not the only one feeling this energy crackle between us.

"The distressed jeans and the hoodie for the first scene, then the button-down and jacket should be for later this afternoon," she says without looking at her notes. And for a second, I see a glimmer of that girl I saw online last night. Confident, charismatic, and passionate.

"Perfect," I say as I turn to head back up the stairs of the trailer, the muscle in my forearm taut as I hold the hangers with two fingers. But before I make the journey, she pulls me back with a question.

"You nervous?"

"About this conversation or the gig?"

"I meant the job. Why would you be nervous talking to me?"

I pause briefly before answering, but figure since she continued this conversation, she won't mind a bit of forwardness. "It's not every day I get the opportunity to talk with such a good-looking woman," I rasp, my hazel eyes dancing with her soft browns.

"In LA, I find that hard to believe," Raven responds. And it's not self-deprecating. No. She doesn't make it sound like she doesn't think she's pretty, which is good because she definitely is and she should know it. It's biting, edgy. A lot like her, I'm coming to find out.

"You're not like most women that I meet here. And that is, if it's not clear by my tone, decidedly a compliment."

"It should be. I'm a catch," she says with a flick of her ponytail.

"No argument here," I say and then my curiosity gets the better of me and I can't help but ask: "But just to clarify, are yeh a fish in the sea? Or have yeh found yerself an aquarium already? Like, there's no question you're a catch, I'm just wondering if you've been hooked?"

Though that analogy played out a little better in my head, she parts those bright red lips in a delicious smile as she answers, point blank, "I'm single if that's what you're asking." And there's that sassiness she put on display Saturday, that playfulness I saw in her TikTok video.

"'Tis. That's exactly what I was asking," I say, returning her smile with a deliberate flash of the tiny dimples hidden behind my stubbled cheeks.

"Well," she draws out the word, "I better keep moving. Still have to drop off of the rest of this rack to the other actors." And even this innocent mention causes my eyes to dart just briefly to pillowy mounds straining the fabric of her ribbed black tank top. My next words are all business, even if the thoughts racing through my mind right now are all pleasure.

"Yeah, the director wants to see me on set before we start, so I'd better get these jeans on and head over, but this has been delightful. Again." We both start to head off, but I just don't want to stop talking to her. So I turn back around, greeted this time by an incredible view of her pert, round ass hugged perfectly in a pair of high-rise Levi's, the little red tag planted on her right cheek like an astronaut's flag, and I can't help thinking that's a land I would love to discover.

"Oh, Raven, one last question," I ask, slipping back into my brogue with ease. "These jeans," I say holding up the pair she handed me. "Did they come this way, or did you turn them from Denim to Daaaaaamn?" I ask, with a sparkle in my eye as realization instantly hits her.

She cants her hip, placing one hand on her slim waist as she asks with a playful hint of challenge, "You big into SewingTok? Or is DIYTok more your scene?"

"Blame the algorithms," I say while thrusting my one free hand up in the air, palm out. "I swear I wasn't trying to stalk you or anything. Just doing some mindless scrolling when I couldn't sleep last night and then a face I recognized popped up and I learned how to distress my own jeans with items I already have around my house."

"Well, that's just something I do on the side," she fires back with a hint of defensiveness, though there's no need in my mind. "Transforming clothes has always been an interest of mine."

"That's grand. I totally loved it," I reply, and though the lilting Irish sound of my voice might be fake, the words I speak to her are very honest. "Didn't get a chance to watch any of the others, but I am now officially a Rags to Raven subscriber."

Her wan cheeks rise on a soft laugh and a smile as she says, "Well, I appreciate your support. See you on set, Liam. And hey," she continues with a serious shift in her tone, "you're gonna be great."

"Thanks," I say as I turn back toward my trailer. And I've never wanted to prove someone right more in my entire life.

Shortly after getting dressed, Jared ushers me over to the set. The crew buzzes around adjusting lights, taping cables to the floor, panning cameras. I walk over to a high-backed folding chair with the *Boise Patrol* logo emblazoned on the fabric. Below that, the word 'Director' is stamped officiously. Dennis Lawson, Emmy-winning director, sees me and grins. "Liam, man. I am thrilled to have you with us."

"Probably not as thrilled as I am to be here. I can't tell you how much this means to me."

"Well, you earned it. That was a killer audition," he says as he pats me on the shoulder. "Listen, before we dive in, I like to check in with some of the new talent. We've got a great team here, so trust the regulars, believe in your gifts, and let's have some fun, yeah?"

"That sounds awesome. I can't wait," I say, having some trouble maintaining my accent because I am so freaking excited right now. I take a steadying breath as Dennis looks over at the set.

"Well, it looks like you won't have to wait any longer. Camera, we ready?" Dennis asks a guy in a gray hoodie and backward Dodgers hat peering through a viewfinder. He gives Dennis a thumbs up and all of a sudden, everyone is in motion.

"Ok," Dennis yells to the room commanding immediate attention. "Actors, let's do places for the top of scene 3b. Let's roll on a rehearsal and see what we get." Then Dennis turns back over to me and lowers his voice to speak directly to me. "Liam, just focus on pursuing your character's objective. Figure out what he wants and go after it relentlessly. Do that and the rest will take care of itself."

It's great acting advice. Hell, it might just be great life advice. I move to my mark as I slip out of one character and into another. Liam dissolves and Clint Rogers takes over. The other actors get set, the crew moves to their positions off-camera and an electrified hush falls over the crowded lot. I've never felt a silence this charged before. That external quiet though contrasts sharply with my internal noise. A feeling of guilt surfaces at the thought that I have not been wholly honest with Dennis, this awesome director taking a chance on me. Not only am I lying, but what if this accent masks the scariest truth, the fact that I might not be any good at this.

Before doubt and anxiety drown out everything else, Gray Hoodie announces "rolling," and Dennis cues us in. "Background," he shouts as extras begin to mill through the space. "Aaaaaannnnnd, ACTION."

Like a flip being switched, those worrisome thoughts fade away, my name on that gold star overshadowing all else.

CHAPTER EIGHT

FEW THINGS IN THIS WORLD CAN SUCK THE JOY OUT OF A PERFECT day like sitting in afternoon traffic on the 405. There's just no earthly explanation for how so many people can crawl so slowly down a highway so massive. Inching past the Getty Center on my way back to Venice, I call Devontay to give him the full report. We'd sent a few texts throughout the day, but once we started filming, I became laser focused. He answers on the second ring.

"Top of the morning to ya,'' he deadpans with no attempt at an accent at all.

"Very funny," I retort.

"So, how'd it go? They gonna let you come back?"

"It went great. I can't wait to get to sleep so I can do it again tomorrow. It's like back-to-back Christmas."

"I'm happy for you, man. You deserve this. Even if you did have to lie to make it happen."

"Not lying, Von. Acting. One man in his time plays many parts," I quote the OG William to my friend, "and this just happens to be one of mine."

"And no one caught on to you? That part of the gig seems to be working?" He asks with a mixture of concern and surprise.

"Seems to be going pretty—"

I'm cut off by the call waiting flash on the phone. My brother's picture pops up on the screen. "Oh, hold on, that's Ryan calling. Actually, let me call you back."

I switch over to the other call and immediately announce, "I fucking killed it, bro!!"

"And you're on speaker, Will," he admonishes as I hear Lexi start giggling from the backseat.

"Language, Uncle William."

"Sorry, Lexi Bean. But there are no bad words, just bad times to use them, and I'm standing by this one. I am *pumped*," I shout to the car.

"Ok, poet-philosopher, as nice as that sentiment is, I'd prefer she not repeat that at her next soccer practice, so cool it with the F-bombs. It went well, though?"

"It did indeed," I coo, slipping into my brogue for this sentence.

"That's fucking awesome," Lexi chirps in response and Ryan promptly groans.

"Lex, language. None of that, sweetie."

"Sorry," Lexi and I say simultaneously, then both announce "jinx," with a laugh.

"Ok, well, we're still on for Trivia Thursday night, right?" He asks.

"Day after I wrap filming. I can't wait, bro. Thanks for the call. Bye, Beans. No cursing."

"Bye, Uncle Will. You got it!" And on that note of pure cuteness, I cut the call and continue my slow descent southbound.

I grab some celebratory Tito's Tacos when I finally make it to National Boulevard. Nothing says congrats on your first professional acting gig like a perfectly constructed beef and cheese taco, lightly deep-fried and dipped into tangy red salsa. Ok, four of them. After that, a little bit of Hulu to let the food digest, then I do a relaxing yoga practice to wind down the day, with a few less twists than I might usually do.

Then I'm off to bed to be fresh for another early call time tomorrow. And even riding high from one of the best days of my adult life, I can't keep my thoughts from traveling back to that one conversation I had with a certain dark-haired beauty. Her infectious energy and cutting attitude instantly bring a smile to my face. As does the outline of her perfect mouth. As I begin to drift off to sleep, I grab my phone and open an app. Maybe I've got time for one TikTok video…

INTERLUDE #2

Get Sold on Being Bold

HEY, NOT EVERY TRANSFORMATION REQUIRES DRASTIC CHANGE. PUT that needle and thread down. Unhand those scissors. Today, we're working with what we already got. You're enough just the way you are. So is your closet! You just need to see something old through new eyes.

Sometimes the best way to bring new life to a piece is simply to combine it with something you might not think it goes with. Don't be afraid to take a risk. Who knows? It might just pay off and get more heads turning your way. Love that plaid skirt? Toss a striped button-down boyfriend shirt on top and see how well they play together. Forget what you learned from your mom. Clothes don't have to match to go together. Your floral blouse can go with something other than a pair of jeans. Just because they sell socks in pairs doesn't mean you have to wear them that way!

A clash can be exciting, maybe a little challenging, but hey, life's too short to play it safe. Mix it up, play around. You'd be surprised what you might find.

CHAPTER NINE

My acting teacher, Lenny Schneider, often tells his classes, "Prepare for everything and nothing can surprise you." Well, no amount of planning could have prepared me for one of the ultimate joys of set life. My name on a star on my own trailer? Epic. My face on film with some of the best names in the industry? Euphoric.

But no one told me about the simple, pure, and frankly transcendent joy of Craft Services.

That's right—the food on set is out of this world. And it's everywhere. Lovingly prepared by professionally trained culinary experts, the day's journey can be told one bite at a time. Breakfast tacos, bagels, granola, coffee, and tea segue into artichoke paninis and turkey melts, with tables full of snacks and sides. As lunch melts into the late afternoon, rotisserie chicken and a vegan bolognese are just two of the incredible options hand-picked and prepared by amazing chefs.

And look, here's the thing. I'm so nervous about the work and so focused on the scenes that I'm barely taking advantage of these rotating smorgasbords. But just knowing that they are always there, being refreshed, updated, and expanded throughout the workday is comforting. Nothing makes you feel like royalty faster than having a stranger prepare food for you that you didn't expressly order off a menu. Well, sitting on a throne with a crown on my head and people bowing before me would probably do the trick, but this is a close second.

These thoughts ping-pong through my head as I'm adding a few choice bites to my plate for a late lunch after finishing one of the biggest scenes I have. Clint, my character, gets busted with over a kilo of cocaine and has some rather choice words for the cops as they're taking him in. The feedback from the cast and crew seemed genuinely positive, so with that weight off my shoulders, I'm treating myself to a little arugula salad with grilled salmon. As I reach over to add a scoop of fresh tropical fruit to my plate, I notice a long, thin hand with striking purple nails grabbing the handle before me. My eyes travel the length of that arm up to the face of its owner, a black-haired vixen that pushes all thoughts of food to the back of my mind. Unless of course Raven was on the menu. That's an all-you-can-eat buffet I'd never want to leave.

We lock eyes, and there is no way I'm the only one feeling this attraction. Her entire face comes to life when she catches sight of me. I pull my hand away from the serving spoon, offering it to her instead. "After you."

"A talented actor *and* a gentleman. The complete package," she says playfully. I can't help but think of one present I'd love for her to unwrap. Those nimble fingers unbuttoning my jeans, her sizable breasts pressed against my chest, her ruby lips on my neck. I'm not sure how long the silence stretches, but I know I've got to say something.

"You think I'm talented?"

"Well, I saw you in that last scene. You were quite convincing. Never thought I'd feel sorry for a low-life drug lord before, but there's something about you..." She leaves the thought unfinished, unfulfilled, but hopeful, promising.

"Everyone's just trying to make their way in the world with the tools they've got," I say of my character, realizing instantly I could easily be talking about myself.

And there is no mistaking the full body scan she gives me as she finally reaches for the fruit to add to her plate. I'm not sure how she manages to do this without spilling because her focus does not leave my body. She drinks me in unapologetically. Her milk chocolate eyes rove over the expanse of my chest down to my abs. Good thing she can't hear my heart and stomach in there because the beating and flipping would be a dead giveaway that I am seriously nervous talking to such an attractive woman. The subtle smirk she floats my way sets me at ease. Although her gaze seemed focused on my body, it felt like she took more of me in, appraised not just my physicality, but my whole spirit with that one look.

Then she asks, "So, I'm totally not supposed to do this, but a few of us C's are going out for a drink tonight, nothing too late, and I thought maybe you'd like to come?"

"I'm sorry, what are C's?" I ask, confusion overwhelming the part of my brain freaking out about the fact that I'm pretty sure she just asked me out. And now my elevated heart rate is a result of excitement, not anxiety.

"Oh, yeah. C is the crew. You're an A, an artist. And it's kind of an unwritten code that the C's and A's aren't supposed to co-mingle." She whispers the last sentence, conspiratorially.

I inch closer to her and whisper back: "I've seen what you can do with a bolt of fabric and some thread. I'd call you an artist."

Her pale skin turns a soft pink, her cheeks like the petals of a rose. And I have to take a small step back to compose myself. Because I want this. I definitely want to see her outside of work, but I've hustled for eight years for this career opportunity. I know I need to stay focused on my character, the scenes, this role, until I wrap filming tomorrow.

So, though it pains me to say it, I politely decline.

"Rave," I start, the shortened version of her name rolling off my tongue like it belonged in my mouth—like *she* belongs in my mouth. "That is an extremely attractive offer from an extremely—well." I cut myself off teasingly. "As much as that sounds like exactly what I want to be doing tonight,

I've got one more day of filming and I just want to stay one hundred percent focused on this. This job is a huge deal for me, and I don't want to do anything to jeopardize this chance."

I can't quite read the expression on her face, so I continue. "I hope you're not mad, I really would love to go. It's just the timing's not the best."

"No, I'm not. At all." She says with a hint of a smile. "I dig how into your work you are. I feel the same way about my career. If something is in the way of my plans, that something is in trouble." She jokes making a karate chop motion with her one free hand.

"Can I get a raincheck, though? I definitely want a raincheck," I almost beg.

She thinks about it briefly, not keeping me in suspense for too long, for which I'm grateful. "Sure. A raincheck. Though it hardly ever rains in LA, so I don't find myself giving these out often…"

"Never stops raining in Ireland, so I'm glad you've made an exception," I say, slipping deeper into this character while at the same time slipping deeper into thoughts of Raven.

CHAPTER TEN

My final day on set lasted the longest. By the time Dennis called the day a wrap at ten o'clock that evening, I felt both exhausted and elated. My first professional television appearance in the can, as they say. With this show's tight turnaround times, my episode is scheduled to air in just a few short weeks. Dennis even pulled me aside before I left to tell me how pleased he was with my work. The day had been such a blur that I didn't have a chance to talk to Raven at all. Which, I realized while driving home, meant I failed to get her phone number to be able to follow up on that raincheck I'd been promised. Because apparently, the world didn't want to give me a day full of joy without slipping in a little bit of disappointment too.

The next morning started with a smoothie and toast, then segued into a marathon training session with Von to make up for the day I'd missed because I was on set.

Though I appreciate the results in my rounded biceps, chiseled forearms, and lean, muscly thighs, I do *not* appreciate the way Devontay goes about getting me there. He's had me doing mountain climbers for so long, that I probably could have summited Mauna Kea by now. Blessedly, my phone rings, offering me a momentary reprieve. My enthusiasm at the interruption wanes instantly when I see the name pop up on the caller ID. A name I'd never seen on an incoming call before. My agent's.

"Shit, Von. It's my fucking agent," I exclaim, trying to catch my breath.

"I mean, you should answer it, dude."

"I'm fucked. She's got to know what's up. Oh man, I'm so screwed."

"I told you, Will. You didn't think this through."

"Yeah, we've talked before. She definitely knows I'm American. What do I do?"

"Madonna's the only American I know who became British overnight. Time to pay the piper, friend," Von responds, his tone indicating he takes no joy being right about all this.

Instantly though, some sage advice from good ol' Lenny Schneider comes to mind. "Act expensively," he says. "Make big, bold choices to create memorable performances. No one remembers the actors who play it safe."

As I click the green accept button, the words pour out before I can think about them. "This is Liam O'Connell," I say, the brogue thick and pronounced. "How can I help you?"

The silence on the line deafens as I stare at Von, convinced this entire charade is about to end just as it's starting to get off the ground.

"Liam, sugar. It's your agent, Molly."

Sugar? One does not normally refer to people as something confectionary if they're about to destroy them. I place the call on speaker so Von can hear the rest.

"Hey there, Molly. Great to hear from you. Everything going ok?" I ask, daring some relief to creep into my thoughts.

"I'm calling about your run on *Boise Patrol,* doll." She speaks in her brusque, no-shits-given way, leaving me no clue about the nature of this update.

I continue to await the guillotine. "What's up? I spoke with the director before I left last night. Seemed like everything had gone well."

"Liam, they loved you," she says and I instantly release a breath knowing now it won't be my last. "And Dennis wants you for a new film he begins shooting next month. The guy they had penned in for the lead was caught on camera at a club yelling some pretty derogatory things about women. To a small crowd of appreciative men. Apparently. So they're in crisis mode. Sending the sides now. You're meeting him and the producers on Monday."

"That's wild news. Awful and gross about that other guy, but—"

"You're breaking out, baby. Dennis is the real deal. Impress him and he can move mountains for you. Nail this audition, kid. It could change your life."

"Um, yeah. That's incredible. I'll start looking it all over the second you send the material my way. Thank you, Molly." My euphoria at both not being caught and catching another break is tempered by a new thought that drills into my mind. My agent hasn't had a passing thought about me since I signed onto her roster.

"Don't thank me, you're the one who did the work," she responds, making it sound somehow like *she* really did do all the work. But before I have a chance to get irritated, she continues. "Oh, one other thing, Liam."

Oh shit, here it comes.

"I don't think I realized you're Irish. I thought you were from Cincinnati."

I look at Von who offers no help, nothing but a hint of judgment. At this point, I'm fully committed to the lie and pin my hopes on her continued indifference.

"Oh, huh. That's weird," I say as nonchalantly as I can muster. "I'm definitely from Dublin. Born and raised."

"Must be another client," she dismisses immediately. Nobody Will transforms into Somebody Liam in real time.

"Yeah, one who's not working," I joke, flying perhaps a little too close to the sun.

She laughs as she says, "Well, that's nothing for us to concern ourselves with, now is it? Knock 'em dead next week."

I meet up with my brother later that night, still riding the high of the news about the producer meeting with Dennis. They say there's no such thing as an overnight success, but this sure does seem to be happening fast. I obviously don't want to get ahead of myself. And I have busted my ass for almost a decade, so this certainly didn't happen overnight. But Liam certainly does seem to have the luck of the Irish on his side.

Or, I mean, I do. I have the luck. Because I *am* Liam. Liam is Will. Will-Liam. That's me. This fake identity thing certainly isn't getting any easier to wrap my head around.

"Hey, space cadet, do you know the answer?" My brother pulls me from my thoughts. We're tucked into a booth at our favorite bar on the east side, Ye Rustic Inn. Sure, it's a shlep to get out here, but this spot has the best chicken wings in town and a super-fun trivia night, so Thursdays I gladly drive the 10 to the 5 freeway to get over to Los Feliz. Plus I've got a good buddy Teddy who lives over here, and he and his girl London usually join us. Not tonight, however. Some sort of private event at the club where he Deejays.

"I didn't hear the question. Sorry," I confess, so my brother then parrots the Literature category stumper back to me. Though I didn't go to college, I've always been an avid reader. Just because I'm not in school doesn't mean I still can't find plenty of ways to keep learning and challenging myself.

When he's finished asking me which author sold over two million copies of one of his novels, *Norwegian Wood,* in Japan alone, I tell him "Haruki Murakami" and he writes it down.

That's the final question in the category and Ryan takes our sheet to the host. He stops by the bar to grab another round of drinks.

When he returns with fresh beers, he withholds mine to force eye contact. "What's going on, bro?"

"I've just been thinking about this audition. Been distracted."

"No," Ryan begins, looking from me to Von. "That's not it, is it, D?"

"Nah," Devontay agrees. "That face he's had plastered on all night. That's not a happy-work-opportunity face."

"It isn't," Ryan picks up. "It's a love-sick-puppy-dog face."

"Ok, guys. Come on. That's insane. I'm not in love. Just been thinking about this chick from set."

"The one who asked you out and you turned down?" Von needles.

"Dude, I was making a responsible decision. This TV show is a huge deal for me."

"You mean, a responsible decision after making the insanely reckless one of pretending to be someone you're not just to get the job in the first place?"

"That's not what I'm doing. I'm just presenting a different side of my own personality."

"Yeah, a more marketable, hirable one," my brother throws in, coming to my defense. I think. I eye him sidelong.

"Well, whatever, dude," Von continues, moving on from this topic. "So, you didn't get her number. You said you found her on the Tok, right? Just slide into those DMs."

Just then the trivia host announces that teams need to return to the table to get their updated score sheets. I make a move to get up for our team as I spy a skinny, black-haired ghost floating to the host table. "Holy shit," I whisper-shout to the table.

"What is it?" Ryan and Von both ask.

"Looks like I won't need to hit her up online. There she is."

My boys both crane their necks in the direction I'm looking and take in Raven's electric energy. "Well, she's hot," Von states immediately. It would seem they also take in her curvy silhouette, inked arms, and dark-as-night hair.

Just as I'm about to rise to go say hi, I freeze. "Fuck," I say in realization. "If I go talk to her, I'm gonna have to put that Irish accent on again."

"Why?" This from Ryan. "The show's over. Just come clean."

"But I've already had like a dozen conversations with her as Liam, and she likes the accent. Like she's definitely complimented me on it. Plus, she works in the industry. Even if we're not on the same show anymore, she knows tons of people that could blow my whole shit up."

Von just sits there smugly, arms crossed over his hulking chest.

"What?" I bite.

"You already know what. I don't even need to say it."

"Yeah, alright." I take a deep breath, steel myself, and walk over to her. She hasn't noticed me as I approach, her face turned away from me, so I sidle up behind her and whisper in her ear with my soft Irish accent, "Pardon me, miss," feigning as though I don't know her. "You wouldn't happen to have an umbrella I could borrow, would you? Forecast is calling for a spot of rain."

She turns around with a wicked grin pulling at her red-painted lips. "Really?" she asks, the devilishness coloring her voice too. "Hardly ever rains in LA."

I can feel eyes on us from every corner of the bar now. Her friends and mine delight in our silent exchange, but we may as well be on an island for all that I can focus on anything other than the fire burning behind Rave's almond eyes.

"No, not really. But you are the prettiest girl in this bar and I wondered if you fancy giving a guy your number?"

She plays along, purring near my ear, "I don't make it a habit of giving my number to strangers."

"A smart rule, to be sure. But perhaps you remember me from, like, yesterday? A few days ago you had a tape measure wrapped around my neck and you were so close to me I couldn't help but inhale your intoxicating scent."

"That's starting to sound familiar. What did I smell like?"

"Burnt vanilla and orange peel. Like an honest-to-God dreamsicle."

I can see the skin on her neck pebble as she takes in my comment and she seems to be digging this more aggressive approach so I add, "And I'll bet you taste even fucking sweeter." The fire is still dancing in her round eyes. Before I lose all my cool and bite into that soft, creamy flesh, I pull back from her slightly with a warm smile.

"I am glad I ran into you. Can't hit you up for that raincheck if I don't have your number."

"That's fair," she says, extending her open palm. I unlock my phone and give it to her.

As she's adding her info, the host announces the scores heading into the final round. "And two teams are tied for sixth place, A Stitch in Time and Boy, See I'm a Hoe both have thirty-eight points…" He continues rattling off the scores, but both of us have stopped listening.

"Are we tied?" I ask her.

"Went with a Boise pun for your team name?"

"It's not very good."

"No, it's not," she agrees instantly.

"Thank you. Hey, I've got an idea. Care to make this final round interesting?"

"What did you have in mind?"

"How about if your team beats mine, we do drinks with your crew, as originally planned. But if my guys can pull it out, then I get to take you out. Alone."

"Like a date?" she teases.

"Exactly like a date."

"Alright, Liam. You're on." She extends her hand to shake on it.

As I get back to our table, grin plastered on my face, the host announces to the room, "Alright folks, the final category for tonight is SCIENCE."

I look at the pair of blank faces staring back at me and exclaim flatly, the brogue melting away with my confidence, "Fuck."

Twenty minutes later, we listen to the announcer rattle off the final tally. "In seventh place with forty-one points, A Stitch in Time. Sixth place with forty-two points, Boy, See I'm a Hoe."

I catch Raven's eye from across the dimly lit space and see a hint of a smile creep across her face. I follow after her to the bar where she's paying her tab so we can settle our own accounts.

"That was a nail-biter," I say, leaning on the bar.

"Sixth place—biggest winner of the night."

"That it is. How's tomorrow night? I don't want to wait another minute to take you out."

"Eager but honest, I like it. Okay. Take me out to dinner," she commands with a mischievous gleam in her eye. "Little Pine, eight o'clock. You call and make the reservation."

Holy shit, that was hot. Her confidence and assertiveness set my whole body on fire.

She brushes a hand over several strands of dark hair that have fallen across her face, and in one fluid motion, she signs her credit card receipt, folds the black book, slides it across the bar, then brushes her shoulder against my chest as she walks out the door.

And I'm left standing there grinning like an idiot, saying to no one in particular, "It's a date."

CHAPTER ELEVEN

WALKING TO THE FRONT DOOR OF LITTLE PINE THE FOLLOWING evening, I pause briefly to fire off a quick email to my acting coach Lenny. I just remembered that I'm missing my scene study class tonight, but I booked my first gig, so I'm sure he'll understand. The last week has been such a whirlwind that it totally slipped my mind. At the full-length glass door, I give myself a quick scan. Unruly wavy hair tamed slightly with some leave-in conditioner and a rough hand tousle? Check. Face freshly shaved? Nailed it. Slim-fit dress shirt with a crisp open collar? Good to go.

Brimming with confidence and excitement, I stride through the door at bang on eight o'clock and check in with the hostess. She informs me that Raven has already been seated and ushers me to the table with a simple "enjoy your meal," as she departs.

Raven stands as I approach and a lump forms instantly in my throat. Stunning is the only word to describe this vision before me. Stunning, like I've just been bobbing in the ocean enjoying a swim and a stingray brushes my leg and jolts me into another dimension, stunning. Her jet black hair is parted down the middle with thick strands tucked behind her ears, cascading down her luscious neck, resting on her collarbone. I resist my immediate urge to run my finger along that neckline before pressing her body against mine and instead opt for planting a cheek-to-cheek kiss on her with my hand resting firmly on her hip.

The little black dress she's wearing has a low scoop neckline inviting my eyes to her ample cleavage. The dress comes down to mid-thigh, showing the perfect amount of leg, her pale skin radiant against the dark fabric. Though her outfit is monochromatic, complete with calf-high black leather boots, her inked arms add color and allure to her entire aura. And the centerpiece of the entire ensemble—those dangerously dark red lips that shoot blood straight to my dick. Those lips might be a deadly weapon. She should have to carry a permit when she wears that lipstick.

"You look a vision," I say when I can find my voice, which is a criminal understatement, but the best I could muster at the moment.

"You clean up pretty nicely yourself, Mr. O'Connell. That shirt manages to highlight those broad shoulders and that sharp jawline at the same time," she says as I pull out her chair to help her back into her seat.

"Well good. Because after that compliment, I now live in this shirt," I reply as I sit opposite her.

Our server comes by to take our drink order and give us a rundown of the specials and menu highlights. "Our menu has been designed for sharing. The chef recommends ordering between two to three dishes per person and splitting everything. The burnt carrots are one of our signature dishes, and I personally love the crispy cauliflower with kimchi aioli. Care for a drink this evening?" He asks as he sets a pitcher of water on the table for us. Raven orders a glass of white wine. I follow her lead and do the same, happy she went with white because red wine teeth on a first date can be rough.

When he leaves, we both reach for the menus and begin to scan.

"So, this place is vegan?" I ask, glancing at the myriad vegetables listed on the page.

"Yeah, hope that's not a problem. Everything here is freakin' delicious."

"No problem at all. I love plants. Are you vegan?" I ask.

"No, just a conscious carnivore. I try to reduce my meat intake and locally source as much of it as I can. Want to be good to the environment, you know? Leave something for the kids to enjoy."

"I like that. Thoughtful. So, any of the kids in this hypothetical future yours?" Something flashes in her eyes at the question. A pain, a secret. I can't tell, but this seems like choppy waters for her.

"Sorry, I should probably at least wait until the wine arrives before I dive in to family planning." I joke to try to alleviate that moment of tension. She smiles, taking the sting out and changing topics of conversation. We explore the menu, easily deciding on several items we can enjoy together, and I have to say, there's something wonderful about finding a person who can share a meal with you. When our server returns with our drinks, we order a bunch of food and then clink glasses in a quick toast. She brings the chilled vino to her mouth and I'm not sure I've ever been more turned on by a beverage in my life. The way those red puckers press against the glass has my mind racing over all the places I'd love to feel those lips on my body. Her next question brings me crashing back to reality though, and reminds me starkly how difficult navigating this date may be.

"So, tell me what it was like growing up in Ireland."

I have to steer the conversation away from my background because I don't want to lie to Raven. Parts of my backstory may not be true, but I still want to give her a glimpse into the real me. I need to reveal as much of Will as I can behind this Liam exterior.

"My mother told me never to talk about myself on a first date. If you start by being a good listener, then she'll have plenty of time to get to know you later," I say, truthfully, sharing actual advice I've received from my mother. She just happened to give that advice to me in southern Ohio, not in the capital of Ireland. "So, tell me about Raven. You said you moved here when you were nineteen, right?"

"Your mom sounds like a smart woman."

"And I'm a smart man for listening to her."

"Indeed," she rasps with a smile. "I'm from just outside Fresno. A

Cali girl, but more rural farm than urban beach. My dreams were too big for my town, so I saved every penny I could for a year and moved here as soon as I could."

"And fashion, has that always been your passion?"

"I have always loved expressing myself through clothing. But costuming is a little different than straight fashion."

"Forgive my ignorance. How so?" I ask, fascinated by her world and drawn in by her enthusiasm.

"They're both about designing and building looks, but costume design has this fundamental storytelling aspect. Fashion design is more about posing questions, challenging perceptions, whereas costume design is all about answering questions. I love solving the puzzles for each character."

"I've honestly never thought about how involved and integral that part of the process is."

"Of course you haven't. You're an A. We C's just stay in the background and do all the hard work while you stand under the pretty lights and get all the glory." She says this playfully, but there's obviously some truth to her words.

"That's the second time you've mentioned this A and C thing. What's that about?"

"Oh, it's just Crew Code. The C's are the Crew Party and the A's are the Artist Party, the talent. On set, it's just this unspoken rule that those parties shouldn't be partying together."

"Well, Clint Rogers is rotting away in a cell in Boise now, so we don't need to worry about him. I'm just glad he came along to introduce us."

Some of our food arrives and the conversation morphs into a series of moans and exclamations as we try everything. Who knew vegetables could have this much flavor?

I do my best to keep the conversation about her which has the double benefit of keeping me from fabricating too much of my past while I also totally dig getting to know her.

An hour later the table is a sea of empty plates and strewn utensils. I've given the server my credit card, but I do not want this evening to end, so I venture for a date continuation. "There's a great little ice cream shop near here. Any chance I can convince you to take a quick ride in my Volvo for a scoop?"

She does not hesitate, clearly having as much fun as I am tonight. "I actually walked here, so as long as you promise to drop me off afterwards, I'm game."

"That works for me," I say getting up from my chair.

"Lead the way, Liam." And for the first time, the different version of my name stings coming out of her mouth. I push that thought aside for now and lead her out of the restaurant. I place a hand on the small of her back as we walk out the door and the contact sends waves of desire coursing through me. Her laugh, the sway of her hips as she walks, the confidence in her posture, everything about Raven intoxicates me.

And then I stop dead in my tracks on the sidewalk.

She turns when she notices I'm a step behind. "What is it?" She asks, closing the distance between us. The streetlamp creates a glow around her skin and a hint of vanilla dances in the air between us.

Our eyes meet and I ask, "What's your last name?"

"What, why? That's pretty random."

"Just tell me. Now," I growl, need coating my words.

"Locke. My last name is Locke. Why did you need to know that right now?"

"Because I only thought it right to know your full name before I did this." Without any further pretext, I bring my hand to the side of her face, and lock eyes with her as my fingers dance along her jaw, behind her ear, and to the back of her head. Then I guide her face toward mine, inching us closer together in an instant, then crash my lips to hers in a kiss full of more desire and lust than I've ever felt before. Her cumulous lips take me in, radiating heat. She pulls her arms around my waist, pressing her soft body against my hard frame, and her tongue searches mine out. Her hands, her lips, her moans all perfectly in sync with my own body, my base desire. Her thigh grinds between my legs and I'm sure she can feel my instantly thickening length.

I bring my other arm around to her lower back to intensify that connection, confirm with my actions that she is right where I want her to be. We drown in each other. I lose track of time. No, that's not quite right. Time loses meaning when our bodies are joined. We stay in this moment, alone together, for several breaths. Finally, on one shared inhale, our mouths gently fall apart as I rest my forehead against hers, both of us opening our eyes slowly.

"That kiss reminded me of you," I rumble to her, our faces still in contact. The world reduced to the millimeters of space between us and nothing more.

"Um, well, that's good," she laughs, "because it was me."

"I know. I mean, you. That kiss felt like only the way you could kiss. Crafted to your personality. Bold, assertive, and full of passion."

"You hardly know me," she challenges, her hands resting just above the high curve of my ass.

"After that?" I question. "I feel like I've never known anyone so well in my entire life."

She rolls up to her tiptoes and presses those ruby rims to mine again. No tongue, but no less full of intensity. "I believe you promised me ice cream, Irishman," she says, our bodies reluctantly separating.

As we move toward my car, I mumble to her, to myself, to the universe, "No ice cream could ever be as delicious as that."

CHAPTER TWELVE

A few minutes later, I pull Rita into a spot on Hillhurst Avenue, and before hopping out to open the door for Raven, I look over at her. She's looking back at me and I say, "Yeah, I just, before we go in, and I was just thinking, like, you know, yep…" and just as a look of amused confusion hits her face, I lean over and plant another kiss square on her. Because well, now that I've experienced that with her, I honestly can't imagine doing anything else. Like what's the point even?

Maybe a *few* things come to mind, now that I think about it…

She returns the kiss as her neck softens and a gentle moan escapes her. My lips buzz on that "Mmmmmm" sound and my cock threatens the integrity of my zipper for the second time in the span of five minutes. Her fingers trace the outline of my jaw and I want her to never stop touching me.

I pull back, take a deep breath, and fucking smile. "Okay, yes. That was exactly what we needed. Well done. Now let me introduce you to one of the best scoops in the city."

Ample Hills Creamery converted a classic southern California craftsman into a playground for dairy lovers. Whimsical cartoons fill the walls of each room and it's impossible to be here and not smile. All of their flavors are delicious, but one is an instant Hall of Famer. I order one cup of the Ooey Gooey Butter Cake with two spoons and we grab a seat on the bench. For a moment, we can almost pretend to be LA homeowners, enjoying an evening on our front porch.

A cheesy grin splits my face at the thought, and at the sound she makes while swallowing her first bite. The noise is deliciously similar to the one she just made in the car. If I were a weaker man, I'd be jealous of the ice cream.

"Liam, this is wildly fucking good."

"And it seems the sticky cake pieces have brought out the potty mouth in you," I laugh.

"You probably should have gotten two of these," she says seriously, taking another bite. And honestly, I'm having a better time watching her eat anyway.

"Oh no, I'm doing you a solid. See, my mother makes me order dessert whenever we go out to eat. She says if I order it, then it's my dessert and I get all the calories. Then she eats it."

"In that case, how chivalrous," she says with a playful bat of her lashes.

"So, tell me one awesome thing," I say, shifting gears.

"What do you mean?"

"I don't know, just like, tell me something cool you did. Or a project you're proud you worked on. I'm having a great time and I want to keep basking in these good vibes."

"Well, last year, I got to work on my first feature."

"Yeah, which one?"

"Dead Things Make No Noise. You heard of it?"

"Shut up," I shout perhaps a little too enthusiastically, the film playing in my head the second she says the name. "You did costumes on '*Dead Things Make No Noise*'? Oh, Stallone was so badass in that film."

"Incidentally, super nice guy too," she says which I love to hear. Not enough of that in Hollywood.

"You either get in this cage or die on that stage," I say in my best Stallone impression which has Raven laughing.

"That's not bad."

"I'm a huge Sly fan. He's like a fine wine. Most of the time—better with age. Sometimes, straight vinegar."

She laughs again "I actually designed the jacket he wore in that film."

"What?" I exclaim even louder than before. "The denim one with the frayed collar that ends up with a bullet hole and knife slashes? That jacket should have been nominated for Best Supporting Actor. Not joking."

Her eyes pop and she busts out into a huge grin. I know it's awful when guys tell women they'd look better if they smiled more, but in Raven's case, it's just plain true. She's gorgeous all the time, but when she smiles, her joy glows and it lights up everything around her.

"That's a really sweet thing to say," she tells me.

"I mean it. Good for you. You're gonna be a fucking star," I announce confidently.

"Well," she fires the word back at me with playful eyes. "Fashion design is my dream. I love working wardrobe, and creating pieces like that is a rare, but incredible experience, don't get me wrong, I love it. But I want to create pieces that define me, not fictional characters. I actually just turned in a portfolio submission for the next OooLaLa Pop-Up event which is this—"

"I totally know about OooLaLa! Von is always trying to get us on the list at their events. It's like a collective of all the best young artists, musicians, and designers in the city. 'Meet Tomorrow's Tastemakers Today.'" I quote the tagline I've seen on their flyers and posts before. "You should totally display the Stallone jacket at your booth."

"Let's not get ahead of ourselves here. I only submitted an application. They still have to say yes, which is a long shot."

"It'll be grand. I'm sure of it."

"So will you, Mr. O'Connell. You've got that thing no one can teach you."

"Oh yeah, what's that?" I ask, loving when she calls me by my last name, my real name.

"Charisma. Confidence. Charm," she tells me candidly. Because this stick of dynamite never seems to shy away from what's on her mind.

"Those are three impressive C words. I like that."

"It's true."

"Could say the same thing about you, you know?"

"Yeah, well, someone's gotta believe in me," she says and that grayness I saw briefly at dinner clouds over her again. "The ice cream's melting," she says, looking down.

"Oh no, this is my niece's favorite part. She calls it the soupy bits," and I spoon some for myself, then dip back into the bowl to give her one last taste too.

Relishing the quiet and the intimacy of these last few moments, I place my finger on Raven's chin and lean in to give her one soft kiss, my lips navigating to that spot between her lips and her cheek. A kiss I hope conveys my interest, but also my patience. My interest in getting to know her. All of her. But my willingness to wait.

My interest in getting to be with her. All of her. But my willingness to wait.

We walk for a bit through the neighborhood, side by side, then arm in arm, then side by side again. Easy, comfortable. I tell her about my phone call with my agent and the audition with Dennis. She seems to genuinely believe in me and care. I've got a great support network in Ryan and Devontay, and I know this is only our first date, but damn, it feels nice to see her rooting for me. Eventually, we meander back to my most trusted lady, Rita, and I swing the heavy metal door open to usher Raven inside.

When I pull up outside her place, a lack of available parking makes this moment more natural for both of us. "I obviously want to come up to your place right now. And I'm sure you'd love that too," I state with a bit of false bravado. Her eyes sparkle. "But there's not a single place to park on this entire street."

"Shame that. Looks like I might have to issue you yet another raincheck, Irishman."

"I wish I could be upset, but LA really could use the rain," I say as we both lean toward the center of the car to steal one more kiss. The first, I hope, of many.

CHAPTER THIRTEEN

THE NEXT DAY I FIND MYSELF COMMISSIONED TO THE FRONT LINES of a monster hunt in my brother's backyard. Lexi and I have magic wand lassos (which are just a couple of sticks we found under a tree) and imaginary super spy binoculars. We tiptoe through the grass until one of us 'hears' something. Then we descend on the invisible monster to learn more about him. So far, we've found three monsters. They have all been furry in varying colors of stripes and polka dots.

"There's another one," Lexi exclaims. "By that bush."

We surround the beast with our lasso wands and pretend to wrestle him under control. "This is a big one," I joke in my best attempt at a Steve Irwin impression. "I'm not sure we can contain him."

Lexi giggles at my rough attempt at an Australian accent, then swishes her stick wand. "Got him," she says proudly.

"Well, what's the report? Is he a friendly monster?"

Lexi nods her head. "Yes, Uncle Will. Another friendly monster."

"That's great. A backyard full of friendly monsters. The citizens of Backyardia should be safe for now."

"Alright you two," Hazel yells from the other side of the yard. "Food's on the table. Wash your hands, then come eat."

Lexi and I waste no time. We drop our sticks, having clearly lost all their magical powers, and get situated for a late afternoon meal.

Once at the table, Lexi raises her milk cup. I follow suit with my Arnold Palmer. As do Hazel and Ryan. "What are we toasting to, Lexi Bean?" I ask.

"To family," she says as we raise our glasses and repeat after her, "to family."

"And also, to my birthday which is only like three and a half weeks away."

We all laugh and dig in. After a few minutes of the kind of silence brought on by a great meal, I applaud the chef as I fork my last bite of fish.

"Hazel, this salmon is incredible. Another home run. My compliments to the grill master."

"Thanks, Will, glad you like it."

"Hey, speaking of home runs," Ryan chimes in. "I've got the company pair of Dodgers tickets for tomorrow's day game, and we can't go. Lexi's got a soccer tournament in the valley."

"Go Purple Unicorns!" Lexi yells enthusiastically, then devours a piece of asparagus.

Ryan laughs. "You said it, kiddo. So, you want?" He looks in my direction.

"Uh, field-level seats in the shade to begrudgingly cheer on the boys in blue? Yeah bro, I want. Thanks!"

"Devontay is gonna be happy to hear from you," Hazel singsongs.

"I'm actually thinking about asking someone else," I reveal.

"Really?" Hazel stretches the word out to emphasize her interest.

"I met a girl. A great one. We met on set and had dinner last night. It was incredible."

"So, you went out already?" Ryan asks. "Look at you go. This is the woman he talked to at trivia on Thursday, Hazel. I think I mentioned it yesterday?"

"Right," she says. "The one that thinks you're Irish."

"There is that," I admit. "In my defense, there wasn't exactly a great time to bring that up. And I did feel like I shared the real me with her last night. There are just certain details I've had to avoid."

"Like your country of origin," Hazel points out.

"The sound of your voice," Ryan piles on.

"And your name," even Lexi gets in on the action, but before we can get any deeper into this topic, Lexi pivots on a dime, a realization hitting her in real-time. "Wait, Uncle Will. If you go to the Dodgers game tomorrow, then you're going to miss my entire soccer tournament."

"That's true. But I'll make sure Ry sends me lots of videos. Sound good, Lexi Bean?"

Her face lights up. "That works for me. But physical attendance will be mandatory for my dragons and dinosaurs birthday party in less than a month."

I laugh at this precocious kid's vocabulary. "It's already on my calendar. Wouldn't miss it for the world."

"You should probably set a few reminders too," she advises.

"It shall be done," I slip into a quick British accent, as I stand and bow to Lexi. "Now," I continue back in my normal voice, "I gotta get home if I'm going to this game tomorrow. I have a big audition Monday and need to get a jumpstart on my lines."

"Tickets and the parking pass are on the kitchen island. Have fun," Ryan says as I float around the table, giving side hugs to the family, and then pull my phone out on the way out the door.

> **Me:** Scored a pair of tickets to the Dodgers game tomorrow. First pitch at 1pm. Please tell me you're free.

A reply comes in before I've even gotten to my car.

> **Raven:** Hey. I assume you meant to say, 'had a great time last night. Can I take you out again tomorrow?'

> **Me:** Yep, yes. That. Damn autocorrect.

I add a shrug emoji and a grr emoji.

She sends back the smile emoji with the blushing cheeks, and that goofy yellow graphic instantly reminds me of the touch of color that warmed her cheeks when we kissed last night.

Raven: That sounds awesome. I'd love to go. Pick me up at 12:30?

Me: I can't wait.

Then I send her a silly GIF of a bulldog in a Dodgers uniform, instantly regret it, but am relieved when the 'like message' notification pops up next to the image. With a smile on my face, I slip my phone into my pocket and drive home.

INTERLUDE #3

Support your Squad in Style

2-4-6-8, WHO DO WE APPRECIATE? THE PERSON AT THE GAME WHO does just enough to zhuzh up that tired team gear into something fabulous.

Everyone loves to rep their squad, but let's get serious, stitches… those frumpy jerseys aren't flattering on anyone, and those baggy tees and sweats might be great for the couch, but they're not getting it done at the park on game day. With a few simple steps and your own signature style, we can turn this home-team jersey into a home run!

For this look, we're going to leave the stitching and patchwork to the big leagues and focus on personalizing this piece with some crystals. Pick a color or pick every color, then make that logo pop with a sparkly outline. Get bold on the back with patterned jewels or go freestyle for an eye-catching look.

Once you're feeling your 'fit, simply layer that jersey over a white or complementary color tank, twist and tie for some much-needed definition, and then it's time to root, root, root for YOU. Because you look fabulous and you're the most important part of your world. Kisses, my stitches!!

CHAPTER FOURTEEN

SUNDAY BEGINS WITH SOME TIME ON THE WATER. SOME MUCH-needed time with my thoughts. I spent the evening working my scene for Monday's audition, so inevitably, part of this quiet time on the ocean means lines running through my brain. As the ocean continues to shift my center of gravity, the board responding to the waves, me responding in turn, I try to bring my thoughts back around to nothingness. Which is a surprisingly difficult state of mind to attain. Who would have thought nothing could take so much concentration? It's additionally difficult for me since visions of Raven keep penetrating my brain. And frankly, I welcome the assault, because even in my mind's eye, I love looking at Raven.

Career, relationships, self-worth. These concepts balance in my brain as my legs try to balance me on the board. I have worked hard for these opportunities. These breaks are the reason I moved to LA in the first place. And Liam isn't make-believe. *He is I and I am him*. My mind jumps immediately from the words of Snoop to that other famous bard, Shakespeare. *What's in a name? A rose by any other name would smell as sweet.*

I don't want to lie to Raven. But on the other hand, there's more to a person than his name and the place he grew up. Some of the career goals I'd set for myself since the day I got here are finally starting to bear fruit. When I talk to Raven about the things that matter to me, share my passions, my hobbies, my dreams. Those aren't lies. That's me. The most authentic version of me. He just so happens to be behind a mask that's helping me achieve some of those very dreams.

Until the time is right. Until I know my career won't be thrown into jeopardy by revealing my true self to Raven, I need to focus on limiting the lies. Maybe I can't tell her about the details of my life before moving to LA, but she can still get a sense of the kind of man I am. The values and principles instilled in me. Whether or not that happened in the Mount Adams suburb or the banks of the River Liffey. That's not as important as the fact that they are who I am. Though my name on her lips is starting to sound a lot sweeter than my name up in lights.

As I breathe out these thoughts and focus on getting ready for the game, my center of gravity shifts, the board titling in the same direction, sending me toppling seaward. I choose not to take that as a sign of anything.

A few hours later I park trusty Rita in Lot G at Chavez Ravine and escort Raven inside the stadium. Raven looks stunning in a bright white Dodgers jersey that she's tied around her midriff. The perfectly placed knot resting on her right hip reveals a hint of her smooth, flat stomach underneath. We slide into the folding yellow seats, shaded from the sun by the Reserve level overhang just as the game gets underway.

"I am embarrassed to admit this," she starts as we settle into our seats.

"Go on…" I cajole.

"But this is my first in-person Dodgers game."

"Well, I am honored to be your first," I say suggestively.

She smirks, then says, "I assume then that this is not your first."

"It is not. Sometimes it's nice to be with someone that has some prior experience, though."

"How much experience are we talking?" And it's clear this conversation has taken an immediate turn.

"Not a lot. I've been to a few games. I think, a reasonable number of games for a man my age."

"Well, that could certainly be a wide range, now couldn't it?"

"I've been to enough that I know my way around the stadium, but I'm still looking for that perfect seat at the World Series. How's that?"

"Good enough for now, Mr. O'Connell," she says as she appraises me.

"In all seriousness, my brother's company gets season tickets. If no one at the agency can go, sometimes I get lucky."

"Fun. So, does that make you a Dodgers fan then? I imagine there wasn't a lot of baseball growing up in Ireland. Although, I honestly have no idea," she says.

And it didn't take long for me to land in some murky water here.

I think back to this morning's session on the water. I dig deep for an honest answer. One that reveals a true concept without revealing false content. "I believe the power of sports revolves around two things: individual human achievement and community pride. So, I feel strongly that people's athletic allegiances should be based on only these two things: a player that demonstrates the limitless potential of the human spirit and where you're from—or where you live. This team has some of the best players in the game and I live here. So, Vamos Los Doyers."

"Vamos, indeed. You have thought that through."

"I guess I have. Never said any of that out loud before, so I didn't know it was in there," I reply with a true hint of surprise in my lilted voice.

We both share a light laugh as I grab us a chocolate malt to share from a passing vendor.

"Here you go. This will keep us cool out here. It's got nothing on Ample Hills, but it's impossible to eat anything with a flat, wooden stick and not smile. I dare you to try."

She takes the offered spoon to her lips, then waits a beat before smiling.

"See, I told you." I go on, and then my face follows the same line that spoon just traveled until I find my lips pressed to hers. Public displays of affection like this haven't always been my thing. But that thought melts away as our lips melt together. After a second of tasting the chocolate on her tongue and feeling the sun-kissed warmth of her lips, I pull back slightly and confess, "I've never been into PDA in the past."

"Me neither," she admits. "That was nice though."

"Now I'm thinking it wasn't that I wasn't into PDA, just maybe I've never wanted to kiss anyone as badly as I want to kiss you."

"Yeah?" she asks, a light pink dusting her alabaster cheeks.

"Yeah." I return with an easy smile and our attention shifts for a while to the game.

A couple innings later, my stomach starts rumbling and I check to see if Raven could eat too. She acquiesces, so we leave our seats and start making our way up the aisle.

"Ok, there are two iconic food items at this ballpark, garlic fries and the Dodger dog," I say as we reach the top of the steps. "We will be skipping the former for obvious lip-locking reasons, but the latter you must try. Insider tip though, at certain kiosks they have a kosher version that's all beef and also way more delicious. If you're game?"

"Let's do it," she says, and I realize one of my favorite things about Raven. That carefree spirit, that willingness to say yes, to try something.

"Great. Follow me."

After procuring what they call the "Brooklyn Dog", we find a high-top table to dig in and catch a little sun away from the game for a minute. We both eat with an aggressive forward lean to ensure no condiments land on our white tops, hers the previously mentioned Jackie Robinson jersey and mine a snug-fitting V-neck tee that I hope shows off some of my definition without seeming like I'm trying too hard.

"What do you think?" I ask as I set my dog down to make sure my face remains as clean as my shirt.

"It's good, but it's a lot. I may not finish this. Don't want you to feel insulted."

"I may not either, honestly. But sharing a hot dog just didn't give me the same Lady and the Tramp vibes as a strand of spaghetti, know what I mean?"

"I think you're spot on there," she says as we both laugh lightly.

"If I haven't said it already, you look great, by the way. And, if I haven't said it, I'd be shocked since I've been thinking it for basically the last two hours straight." Then I stop myself from rambling further. Rambling, incidentally, that seems to flow easier with the Irish accent.

"You did not, so thanks," she says, brushing a cluster of straight black locks from her face. "You do too. Infuriatingly."

"What? Why is that infuriating?"

"Because all you had to do was grab a tee-shirt and a slim-fit pair of jeans and you look delicious. Women, meanwhile, have three different drawers for different kinds of tops based on style, season, outfit, and comfort, not to mention the accessories and all the rest."

"First of all, let me pause to relish the fact you just called me delicious."

"Ew," she interjects. "Did you just drop a hot dog pun in on the convo?"

"That was an accident, I swear. Relish comment rescinded," I say, miming putting the words back in my mouth. "To get back to your point, I did think about putting on a watch, but was afraid I'd bang it against a metal seat. If that makes you feel any better," I say sheepishly.

"Oh, don't get me wrong. I love getting dressed. I love clothes, obviously. I just think it's incredible how little men can get away with, especially when you consider that it's the exact opposite in nature."

"What do you mean?" I ask, digging that fire in her eyes when she talks about one of her passions.

"Male animals often have to use flash to attract mates. Think about it. Peacocks and their plumage; ladybugs and their spots, cardinals and their vibrant red color."

"Wait, aren't all cardinal birds red?" I interject.

"Nope, only the men. The women are gray. The prettier sex in the animal kingdom is almost always the male of the species. Meanwhile over in *homo sapiens* land, we're still trying to teach our men not to wear a brown belt with black shoes."

"Come on, guys know that much!" I defend.

"You'd be surprised," she says with a smirk and takes one final bite of her hot dog before wrapping the rest up.

The sound of the organist queuing up *Take Me Out to the Ball Game* pulls my focus. "Hurry, you can't miss your first seventh-inning stretch." And we hightail it back to our seats just as the crowd finishes the second refrain.

Slightly out of breath, we laugh. "Well, I blew it. I have been a poor steward of this experience. I apologize."

"I am not sure I will ever recover from this letdown. Maybe we should just go home?" She offers and there is no getting around her super flirtatious tone.

And this time it's my turn to ask, "Yeah?"

To which she replies by taking a half step closer to me, pressing her breasts ever so slightly against my midsection, looking up, and whispering, "yeah."

And as far as I'm concerned, that, ladies and gentlemen, is the ballgame.

CHAPTER FIFTEEN

I PULL UP HER STREET, HAVING BEATEN THE HORRIFIC END-OF-GAME traffic leaving the stadium, and the parking gods have seen fit to bestow upon me a spot directly out front of her place.

"This is me," she says pointing at a Spanish-style duplex with a high beige archway. "You did find a spot to park, so…"

"Would love to cash in that raincheck," I say leaning over and planting a confident kiss on her lips. "I do have a huge audition tomorrow, so I can't make it a late night, but I would love to see your place."

"Come. On. Up." She says, punctuating each word as she pops her car door open and scurries up the steps ahead of me. Not gonna lie, I could get used to the view from here, as I'm slowly hypnotized by the gentle sway of her ass.

When I regain my wits, I follow behind her and reach the landing as she's opening the front door. "Welcome to my home," she says by way of invitation, and I'm greeted by a flood of light and color as I walk into the space. The walls vibrate with vibrant hues from mosaic tile artwork and bright prints, while every corner of the naturally lit space is adorned with a potted plant or flower. The space transports me to a beachside art gallery.

"Whoa. This room is like a living, breathing thing," I say, taking it all in.

She laughs dismissively. "There are a lot of plants."

"I love all the natural light. What they are, are happy plants."

"Hey, if you're gonna live in a place that's sunny basically every day, may as well celebrate it."

"Exactly why I live so close to the beach. It costs a lot, but some things are worth the effort, know what I mean?"

"I do," she replies.

"Love that Shepherd Fairey print, too," I say, my eyes resisting the urge to look at anything but Raven. I'd not seen this tiger print before, but the lines and industrial print style are unmistakable.

"It's my roommate's," she says, "but I dig it too. They went to the same high school in Idyllwild, so she loves collecting his stuff."

My attention is thrown by the dreaded R-word.

"Roommate?" I ask suggestively.

"Yes, but she is currently on a mushroom tea excursion in Joshua Tree and won't be coming back until Tuesday."

"If she makes it back at all," I joke.

"Willow is a very free spirit," Raven tells me.

"To each their own. No judgments here," I say with my palms raised.

"I'm sorry. I'm being rude. Did you want something to drink?" She asks, making her way toward the kitchen, and I take one long stride to reach her and place my arm around her stomach, pressing my body flush against her back.

"I hope I'm not being rude when I tell you the only thing I want is standing right in front of me," I whisper hungrily into her ear, and I swear I can feel the butterflies dance in her stomach. She turns her body toward mine, my hand never leaving her bare midriff, and when her face reaches mine, we kiss. We fucking consume each other. Her hands press firmly into my muscular back and my left hand comes to her cheek as she devours my lips, then kisses her way down toward my neck.

A throaty "mmmm" escapes me, a sound I've never made with this much clothing on before. On her next inhale, she burrows her nose into my neck, her fingernails clawing the fabric of my shirt. Then she pulls her eyes up to mine. "You smell like tobacco," she says huskily.

"You saying I smell like cigarettes?" A light laugh comes out on this line, but it does not dissipate the intensity of the moment, if anything it strengthens the intimacy. "Most people think that's gross," I continue.

"No, you smell like a tobacco leaf before it's burnt. Strong, earthy. It's intoxicating," she rumbles as I come unglued.

"Better not burn me then," I growl as I press her body impossibly closer to my own, run my hand up her back, and claim her mouth. Claim all of Raven.

After several breaths of easily the best kissing of my life, I take a cue from the clawing she's been doing to my back and pull away long enough to drag my white tee over my head. She takes a moment to appreciate my body as her hungry eyes devour the contours of my waist, the definition of my stomach, the sculpt of my chest.

"Your body's already on fire," she says, and the way she says it has my cock straining impossibly against my jeans. The lust dripping from those two little syllables. Fire.

"Which one of these is your bedroom?" I ask pointing to the two closed doors on the other end of the living room.

"That one," Raven points, and instantly I scoop her up from behind her thighs and carry her that way.

Once we're on the other side, I kick the door closed behind me, then toss her back on the bed. Her butt bounces on the down comforter, then she swivels around and springs to her knees with the grace and speed of a puma. And all I can think is *come here, kitty.*

But before either of us pounce, I bore my gaze straight into hers and tell her, "Take that top off for me."

She looks back at me with nothing but playful challenge in her heady gaze. "Take those pants off for me," she purrs.

Without so much as a shift of my eyes, I bring my hands to my waist and begin unfastening my belt. As I do, she brings her hands to the knot above her hips, unties it, and lets the jersey hang. Then she expertly unclasps each button before gliding her hand up the center seam to expose her pale, smooth skin. My eyes wander to her creamy tits held in place by a white lace bra as her eyes take in the bulge currently reshaping my boxer briefs. She pulls the jersey off behind her and drops it to the floor. As the white cotton floats to the floor, like a driver being given the starting flag, I approach. Placing a firm hand on her shoulder, I lay her flat on the bed as her black hair pours over her pillows.

"I will take care of these," I say, fingering the button of her jeans as I press my body atop hers and begin drowning her in kisses. My turn now to take soft bites and delicious tastes of her neck, as my other hand takes firm grasp of her breast. As sexy as the lace is, right now, I see it as nothing but an impediment to another part of her I need to explore. So, with her jeans unbuttoned, I bring my other hand up and arch her back to unclasp the bra, then peel it from her body.

Too lust-drunk for words, I take hold of both her mountainous breasts before descending like an intrepid trailblazer to the unspoiled valley between them. I begin peppering that pillowy softness with kisses, sucking, and nibbling on one pebbled nipple as my thumb grazes and teases the other. Her moans and her grinding into my hip tell me that she's enjoying this too, which is good because I'm not sure I ever want to stop.

With lustful attention paid to both tits, I travel further down her body, greedy now to explore every inch of her. My stubbly chin scratches her delicate flesh as my mouth follows behind to kiss every available inch of her. The tiny, soft hairs on her belly rise as I continue my descent, my hands having made quick work of her zipper. As I lift up on my knees to pull her pants down, I make sure to take her panties with them, unable to wait another second to know all of her.

And when I see her there, laid bare, a dark strip of hair offset by an ocean of soft creamy white skin, I want to drown in her.

"I can't get over how pale your skin is. Like snow," I say reverently, as I caress her hip, my thumb dancing near her inner thigh.

"I know, it's pretty ridiculous to be this pale in a place this sunny," she says with one of the first hints of self-consciousness I've seen from her since our first meeting.

"No, I fucking love it. You're like a swan swimming in a sea of geese. Beautiful," I say as I lay a kiss just above her pubic hair. "Enchanting," I say as I kiss inside one thigh, my other hand inviting her to open for me. "And unique," I growl as I kiss the top of her mound, laying wet, tongue-soaked kisses on her clit.

"Be careful. Swans are notoriously aggressive, and have been known to bite," she purrs as she squeezes her thighs playfully against the sides of my head.

I lock eyes with her over the contour of her body, then nibble teasingly at her inner thigh. She smirks as her head rolls back and her legs part invitingly. I devour these sweet lips with the same hunger and ferocity with which we were kissing earlier. My mouth and tongue make reverent work of every inch of her wetness. When I feel her arousal rise, as her hips begin to buck toward my mouth, I bring the pad of my thumb around to massage slow circles on her clit while my tongue does laps at her entrance. As the pace of her thrusts picks up and her moaning intensifies, she brings a hand down to grip the back of my head. My hand slides around to the back of her ass as she finds a way to take some control, gliding her cunt up and down my mouth. I part my lips, pressing my tongue fully against her center as she grinds into me.

"Fuck, Liam. Your tongue feels so fucking good. I'm gonna come."

I moan ravenously into her, sending vibrations coursing through to her clit. Then pull off her just far enough to growl into her pussy, "That's what I want, Rave. That's all I want. To see you come." With my hands now both full of her pert ass cheeks, I press myself fully to her and lap up and down her slit, applying constant pressure to that sweet fucking cherry on top.

And within seconds, she loses control and erupts for me—her hands slamming into the comforter on either side of her, ass cheeks flexing in my rough grip, and creamy thighs quivering around my head as she does as promised and comes for me.

Her undulations slowly subside and her breathing evens out. I lift myself up asking, "Do you have a condom?"

"Top drawer, dresser." She mumbles as she points to a chest on one side of the room.

I quickly slide off the bed, removing my underwear in the same motion, then rip the seam off the prophylactic.

As I ready myself, she starts to sit up, looking a little dizzy but still very seductively asking, "Can I return the—"

I cut her off before she can finish the thought. "Next time," I assure her. "And you won't have to ask me, but right now I need you to lay the fuck back down and let me feel just how wet I made you."

She promptly complies, and I seat myself between her legs again, tapping her clit lightly with my rock-hard shaft before taking one luxurious stroke of my sheathed cock down her clit, parting her slit with my tip, then slowly but steadily driving myself home.

As we take each other in, inch by glorious inch, our eyes lock. I feel her walls grip my length as I continue to fill her—no retreat, just a singular, welcomed invasion. One penetrating stroke. "Very wet," she whispers as she pulls my face to hers.

"Very wet, indeed," I repeat, as she slides her tongue into my mouth while my dick slides deeper into her. Once fully seated, I flex my ass to drive just that much deeper as she releases a moan that shoots sparks down my thighs.

We immediately find a rhythm. Our bodies cling desperately to each other as I pound into her in long, languid strokes. Like a train leaving the station, our breaths, our moans, and our hips all pick up pace evenly. Her breathy 'aaahs' meet my throaty 'mmmms' as we slide closer together, then farther apart, but never fully separated.

"You feel really fucking good, Liam," Raven moans to my lips.

"I was about to say the very same thing, Rave," I grunt out as the sensations begin to take over my brain and body.

As I near that moment where pleasure will overtake everything, this dark little bird beneath me catches my eye, then flips me over in mid-thrust, her wide hips capturing me, a predator atop her prey. But I am only too happy to be devoured. She smirks proudly at this shift in position, then lets out a sigh as her back arches, her body finding even more of my length as she grinds into me.

Her tits bounce freely now as she relaxes into this, very much enjoying the ride. And I am too; I don't want her to ever get off.

Well, I do…

With that in mind, I try to seize control back by pawing her ass cheeks and jackhammering into her from below. Her hair dances around her head as her mouth falls open on a stuttering 'ohhhh'. Her moan is punctuated by the impact of my pelvis against her core.

After several seconds, she regains control by dropping her weight on top of me and raking her hands across my chest. The sensation feels like a million thumbtacks lightly pricking every inch of my body. I lose myself in the feeling as she seats herself atop me again, massaging my dick at her own pace.

Under her body and under her spell, I give in to Raven. She explores the length and rigidity of my shaft from so many angles as she rides out her pleasure. When her hand finds its way behind her and she grabs my balls, drenched deliciously in her arousal, I fall over the edge and give in to my own bliss.

"Oh fuuuuuuuuuuck, Rave. I'm gonna come," I grunt out seconds from climax.

"That's what I want, Liam. Come for me," she throws my words back at me.

And as I feel the tingling at the base of my neck, I plead, "Come with me, Raven. Please. Come. With me," and on that hopeful wish, I release. Her lithe form above me, her powerful hips around me, and her tight pussy enveloping me, I tense from my calves through my quads as ecstasy pours forth. My cock jerks and spasms inside her as Raven cries out, "Yes, Liam. Right. There. Fuck. You."

And we both devolve into sputtering wrecks. Her heaving tits fall against my firm chest as our labored breathing falls in sync and we come back to earth together.

Slowly, rapturously.

With her head resting against my neck, her hair spilling onto my shoulder, and our bodies still beautifully intertwined, I realize we've not come back to earth. At least not the same earth as before. Because this earth has rotated into something new, something wonderful, something…

Before I can sink any further into those thoughts, the warmth of her body against mine, the calm of this post-coital bliss takes over and my eyes flutter closed.

I do not know if I'm asleep for fifteen minutes or fifteen hours, but my eyes jolt open on a rush of air. Dusk paints the sky outside her window a sea of purple, pink, and reds. While this little blackbird still rests quietly on my shoulder.

The dual realities of my audition tomorrow and a sticky condom invade my mind simultaneously. I gently slide my chest out from under Raven who moans peacefully as I lay her back down while heading to the bathroom. I splash water on my face, clean up, then head back to her room where I am greeted by her gorgeous form still languorously spread across the bed. Like a cup of cream in a black pitcher, Raven's dark comforter envelops her pale skin. And I could drink this in all night long.

"Can I get you anything?" I ask as she wraps the covers over her, opening her eyes slightly.

"Can you go through the house and set all the clocks forward four hours, so I don't feel guilty about falling asleep at 6 o'clock?" She jokes drowsily.

"I can pull those blinds shut if you want," I offer, slipping my pants on as I slip back onto the bed with her.

"Are you leaving?

"I do not want to."

"Sushi and a true-crime documentary?"

"But I have to," I say over top of her words. "Although, that sounds like a grand end to a pretty tops day."

"Why say no when it feels so good saying yes?" she purrs.

"Wait. Was that like the sexiest version of a *Tommy Boy* quote I've ever heard in my life?"

"I'm a classic SNL junkie. Did you ever think Brian Dennehy could turn you on?"

"I most certainly did not," I laugh. "Unfortunately, I have a huge audition tomorrow. Well actually, it's a straight to director callback for Dennis for the lead in a feature, so I really need to get home to rest and focus."

She sits bolt upright in bed, eyes alight. "Liam, that's fucking awesome. Now it is my pleasure to kick your beautifully sculpted ass out of my house. You've got a role to win," she announces enthusiastically, rolling the comforter away from me and sending me to my feet off the side of the bed.

"Thanks for understanding, Blackbird," the nickname flies out of my mouth before I've had a chance to even think it. From the softest lift of her lips, I can tell thankfully that she does not hate it.

"Of course, Liam. I want all your dreams to come true."

After sliding my shirt over my chest, I lean onto the bed and plant a firm kiss squarely on her mouth. "That's an incredible thing to say. I hope you'll let me make this up to you."

"Nothing to make up, Liam. Just go knock them dead tomorrow."

I pause at her bedroom door and look over my shoulder. "Oh, one last thing," I begin. "Is it really perfectly sculpted?" I ask, canting my hip and placing a hand on one butt cheek.

Her eyes travel down hungrily, but she grabs a pillow and throws it my way, laughing. "Get out!" She shouts playfully.

I let the melodic sound of her laughter carry me through her living room, then float to my car.

CHAPTER SIXTEEN

THE NEXT MORNING, I FIND MYSELF IN THE LOBBY OF A CASTING OFfice in Santa Monica, trying desperately to keep my nerves in check. The biggest audition of my career waits on the other side of that beige door and it is hard to stay in control of my emotions.

"Be the answer to their problem." I silently repeat another mantra from Lenny. "Walk into every room like you're here to save the day. They're looking for someone. They have the need. I'm that someone. I fill that need. You're welcome."

After sending that silent prayer up to Dionysus, I send another one specifically to Dennis for my continued duplicity. After tamping that guilt down, I grab the silver door handle and walk confidently into my future.

"Liam, great to see you," Dennis announces the second I make my way through the door. "This is the Madhouse Pictures creative team. I've shown them some of the dailies from your *Boise Patrol* episode and they loved what they saw. Any questions about the sides?"

"I'm thrilled to be here. Great to meet you all," I begin, slipping into

Liam's voice like a well-worn glove at this point. "If you don't mind, could you give me a bit of context for this scene? Where are we in Jett's story at this point? It wasn't quite clear from the pages I received."

"Of course, great question, buddy," Dennis happily responds, sitting closer to the edge of his seat on the couch. "So, Jett's just gotten back to town. We've seen him in hiding, and he's just decided to come claim what he believes is his. That starts with Ruby, his ex-girlfriend that he left in the middle of the night to, in his mind, protect her from the trouble following him."

"Yeah, grand. That's very helpful."

"Alright, Liam. Well, this one is just your monologue, so whenever you're ready," Dennis sits back while I take a deep breath and ground myself. Liam fades away on an inhale, Will enters on an exhale, and when I open my eyes, Jett pours from my bones while a water bottle on the edge of a table becomes my sightline for his one true love, Ruby.

"The only place I've ever felt at home was in your arms. The only place I've ever felt whole was in your bed. You're the only family I've known. The only love I've known. And before you tell me to fuck off. Before you tell me to go away, please let me explain. I was in trouble, Ruby. Am in trouble. So, I ran. I ran away to protect you. To shelter you from my darkness. I couldn't tell you where I was going; the less you knew the safer you were. But I realized something this past month. Alone in that cabin. There's no point in running from my death when I'm not really alive unless I'm with you. I thought I was afraid of the Black Angels. I thought I needed to find a way out of this mess. But the only thing I'm truly afraid of is being without you. And the only way out of this situation is with you by my side. So, I'm sorry, Ruby. I'm sorry for leaving and I'm sorry for coming back. But if you feel even a tenth of what I feel for you then you'll kiss me right now, pack a bag as fast as you can, and come chase death with me."

My eyes haven't moved an inch from their spot, boring a hole into the top of a sixteen-ounce Arrowhead water bottle. My heart races and tears well in my eyes. My feet vibrate with intensity through this pause.

I take one sharp breath in before delivering my final lines. "Well, Ruby? What do you say? Say something. Anything. As long as it's yes."

I hold the final moment for the impact of the scene and also for myself. Just as I start to break character, morphing out of the scene and back into this other scene, Dennis shoots up from the couch. "Holy fucking shit, Liam. That was fucking brilliant. Jesus Christ, man. Where did that come from? First take? Come on!"

I scrub my hands over my face and comb back my wavy hair as I respond in my Irish brogue, "Thanks, man. That felt real nice. Hope you liked it."

"Liked it? We loved it. Liam, you're a fucking marvel. Forgive all the fucking cursing, but I mean, fuck. Great job, man. No notes. Get out of here. Tell your agent to keep her phone on."

Dennis looks around the room to ensure the producers share his enthusiasm, which they seem to do. As much as producers enthuse about anything, anyway.

I head straight to my car, pulse pounding. After a couple enthusiastic hollers and aggressive love taps to Rita's steering wheel, my hands settle down enough to grab my phone. Body buzzing, my instincts cry out to text Raven, but before I hit send on the hastily typed message, I take a deep breath. *Let's not get ahead of ourselves, Will. With Raven or with this movie.* I toss the phone into the passenger seat without hitting send, then drive to Venice for my much-needed session with Devontay.

"You have had yourself a busy twenty-four hours, my man," Von deadpans as he throws my legs toward the ground in one of his many torturous ab-sculpting exercises. "You killed at an aud, crushed with the lady, and saw the Dodgers win their tenth straight at home."

"Well, we technically left before the ninth, so..." I let the sentence hang, unfinished. He punctuates his displeasure with a firm shove of my outstretched legs toward earth for something like the ten-thousandth time.

"Sacrilege, man."

"Dude, I know. But seriously, worth it. Very, very, worth it."

Von finally shows mercy on my body, calling out time after one final push of my legs. My core relaxes as my feet rest on the grass. I roll over into a cobra stretch as Von makes some notes on a chart he keeps of his clients' reps and progress.

"So, when will you know more?" he asks, looking up from his journal.

"About the audition or the girl?"

"I meant the audition," he drones. "Sounds like you already know more than you're letting on about Raven."

"I know I want to see her again, but aren't I supposed to wait like three days or some shit?"

"Dude, what are you, nineteen? Fuck that noise. You like her. You ask her out again. Don't string her along any more than you already are, you leprechaun."

At Devontay's reminder of the mask I'm still wearing with Raven, my stomach tightens. And this feeling isn't brought on by the crunches.

"Yeah, totally. You're right," I say, slightly deflated. "Gotta come correct with the date suggestion though."

"You're on your own there, buddy. If it's not an underground hip-hop show or cage fighting in Boyle Heights, I can't help you out," Von shrugs.

"Hard to believe you're still single," I fire back at him as I grab my bag and head out, my mind already running through a million date possibilities.

Once home, I get showered and changed, then I spend more time than I care to admit finding a perfect outing for me and Raven. When I come across an outdoor screening of *Bridesmaids* at the Hollywood Forever Cemetery tomorrow night, I scoop up a pair of tickets before I've even texted her. Some might call that presumptuous, I call it manifesting my reality.

My overconfidence is rewarded by an enthusiastic text exchange with Raven who tells me she's been dying to see a film there and that she'd go just to see Kristin Wiig and Maya Rudolph, even if she didn't want to see me. (Which, she assures me, she does.) We finalize the details, then I end our chat with one of those side-face kissing emojis which is met with a blushing smile emoji in return.

And I'm reminded how gorgeous her face looks when laughter or lust paints her pale cheeks red. The mental image sends blood rushing faster throughout my entire body, and my mind is overcome with thoughts of Raven. Worry about the outcome of the audition fades away as visions of that blackbird fly through my head. I let those thoughts take me as I drift off to sleep.

INTERLUDE #4

Black is Back / Little Black Dress

OK, MY STITCHES. SAY IT WITH ME NOW. WHAT ARE THE THREE ESsentials for every woman's closet? 1- a great fitting pair of jeans; 2- a signature blazer; and 3- that's right. A little black dress.

That one dress you can wear to Any. Fucking. Thing. It dresses up, it dresses down. It works whenever you need her. From dates to funerals, she's got you covered. She's like your superhero secret weapon. Even when someone sees it coming, they're powerless to defend against it.

So, we need to talk about how to elevate and personalize that centerpiece for every occasion, for every personality.

Once you've found that dress that hugs you in the right places, reveals your favorite parts, and makes you feel like the goddess you are, it's time to take it to the next level with the accents and accessories that make it your own.

Maybe this is your chance to wear that funky headband that you love but can't seem to find an outfit for. Or maybe tonight's the night you bring back slap bracelets?

Or, my personal favorite, draw some tasteful attention to your stems with a pair of vibrant leggings. Bonus: you can add a flash of tasteful color without flashing anyone at a restaurant. And voila, stitches… now THE little black dress is YOUR little black dress.

CHAPTER SEVENTEEN

THE WAITING IS THE HARDEST PART. TOM PETTY'S A FREAKIN' GENIUS, no two ways about it. Waiting consumes my Tuesday. Waiting to hear from my agent, waiting for my date with Raven, just waiting. The frustration is compounded by that total lack of control. I know I nailed the audition, Dennis made that wildly clear. But that still doesn't mean the role is mine. Casting decisions hinge on so many variables that are beyond an actor's control. So, what can I do about it? Nothing but wait.

Did I do my due diligence to lock down a killer date plan with Raven? Yeah, I think I did. Will that result in a smooth evening? Won't know until it happens. Nothing left but to wait on that, too.

"Number fourteen," the guy in the white apron behind the deli case intones for what, based on the hint of annoyance in his voice, is probably not the first time. I glance down at the red chit in my hand with a 14 stamped on it, then hold it in the air.

"Yeah, that's me. Sorry," I say, shaking myself out of my stupor and focusing on the rows of pre-made salads, pastas, and sides in front of me. I order a few items for tonight's picnic dinner date, along with a demi-baguette and some cheese. Raven offered to bring a bottle of wine, so I grab a couple cans of seltzer and a box of Raisinets to complete our dinner and a movie basket.

With everything safely stowed in an insulated bag, I make the drive crosstown to meet Raven at the venue which is just a few minutes from her spot. If my feelings for Raven weren't already starting to become clear in my mind, the number of trips I've taken East on the 10 to see her at this point would be a pretty strong sign that this might be serious. Dating outside your zip code in Los Angeles is not for the faint of heart.

Walking toward the entrance to the venue, bag and blanket in hand, I spy Raven instantly in a crowd of moviegoers. It's not just her neon pink lace leggings that make her stand out, though those certainly do catch my eye. From the soles of her well-worn Doc Martens to the playful twists in her hair, Raven radiates confidence. Her little black dress might look simple on someone else, but on her, it hugs, squeezes, and curves perfectly with her body, demanding my attention. As do the partial sleeves of tattoos, the dark ink dancing off her light skin.

"That dress is so pretty, it makes my stomach hurt," I say when I get close enough for her to hear me. I wrap an arm around her waist and pull my body flush against hers with a firm kiss on the side of her lips.

She leans into the kiss, then rests her forehead against mine. "Did you just start our date by quoting the movie we're about to see?" She whispers conspiratorially.

"Maybe. Too much?"

"I like that you're trying. It's a good look on you. As is this cardigan you've got going on here," she says, fingering the outline of my slate gray two-button sweater. "Shows this chest off quite nicely, which is good because this chest deserves to be admired."

"By you or everybody?" I ask as she tiptoes her fingers along my pecs.

"Oh, it would be selfish of me to hide this from the world. They can look, just can't touch."

"That works for me," I hum as we slowly separate. "You got the wine?"

She pulls a bottle and two plastic cups from her oversized purse. "You got the food?" She asks as I hold the insulated bag out by my fingertips.

"Then let's go find ourselves a seat," I say. "After you."

"What a gentleman," she smiles as I show our tickets to the gate check girl on our way in.

"Wish I could take credit for that one, but honestly, I just like stealing glances at you from behind."

She laughs lightly as I sidle up next to her, running my arm around the back of her waist, resting my palm tastefully, but assertively on top of her round ass.

We find a nice spot to lay out our blanket at the perfect distance from the screen. We've arrived early enough to beat the rush and enjoy the sunset with some food before the film starts. The giant projector screen sits in front of a row of palm trees. A preshow DJ spins ambient lo-fi as the sky does its nightly dance from clear blue caterpillar to multicolored butterfly before turning black for the night.

"So, what do we have here?" she asks as I lay out our spread and hand her a plate, napkin, and utensils.

"I'm still not one hundred percent sure what food you like, so I went to the deli counter at Gelson's and grabbed a little of everything."

"Gelson's?" she asks with mock haughtiness in her voice. "You fancy?"

I laugh as I defend myself. "Yes, as a supermarket that place is insanely expensive, but their deli counter is legit and I not so secretly want to impress you, so here we are."

"Here we are indeed," she says with a twinkle in her brown eyes. She twists the cap off the wine and pours us both a glass.

"Twist-off. Smart move," I say of the bottle.

"This is not my first rodeo, Irish," and the nickname hits me in all the places. I love the familiarity and playfulness of it. The effortless way it rolls off her tongue. But I hate the lie it reminds me of that sits at the root of our relationship. A lie I'm feeling more caged by with each passing minute.

"Slainté," I say, raising my glass since the Irish thing is front and center in my mind.

"To Jessica's Crunchy Kale Salad," she toasts with a question in her voice.

"Ah, a Gelson's aficionado," I say commenting on her first-name-basis reference to an item on the menu. "And yes, there's some right there." I point with my glass, then clink plastic with her.

We drink and share a light meal while I find any excuse to touch Raven's hot pink covered knee or bare, abstractly tattooed arm. She melts into the contact as I try to learn more about her past. She reminds me she's a Central California kid, having grown up just outside of Fresno.

"My parents never had any extra money. We were never food insecure or anything like that, but every paycheck was budgeted. Most of my clothes were either hand-me-downs from Mom or Goodwill."

"Yikes, not sure I'd want to be wearing my mum's old dresses."

"That would certainly be a look," she jokes, eyeing me up. "Though honestly, you've got a body that might just be able to pull that off."

"Yeah, but I couldn't afford the therapy," I retort as a lightbulb goes off in my head. "Is that why you love fashion? Repurposing clothes?"

"You got it. The only way for me to make my own identity was by re-visioning someone else's stuff. It wasn't just necessary, it became empowering. Like I didn't need money, just creativity and a pair of scissors, and I could turn someone else's trash into my treasure."

As Raven lets me into this part of her story, I get swept up in the passion of her voice, the energy pulsing off her as she gets more animated while speaking. Then she becomes uncharacteristically self-conscious and pulls back into herself.

"Sorry, I didn't mean to get wrapped up in my own thing there," she dismisses.

I take her hand as I reply to emphasize my earnestness. "Don't apologize. I fucking love seeing you talk about this. Your enthusiasm is contagious. This was all the impetus for your TikTok channel too, yeah?"

"Rags to Raven," she smiles shyly. "Yeah. If I can help another person on their journey of self-discovery without an AmEx card, that's awesome. I'm really into the ecological footprint of repurposing clothes too."

"What do you mean?" I ask.

"Just like, how much energy can be saved by wearing clothes for more than a few months. Reducing the waste in landfills, keeping kids out of sweatshops. But I don't want to sound all holier-than-thou or anything. I love H&M as much as the next person."

"Yeah, don't ruin H&M for me, please."

She giggles. "Just trying to find small ways to do my part."

"I love it. That's super thoughtful," I say, very into how open and selfless Raven is.

"Plus, it's fun to play around with different styles and trends that have already had their moment," she says deflecting some of that serious energy. "Turn them into something new."

"Remixing clothes. You're like the DJ of the dressing room," I say, then make some record-scratching sounds. "Ladies and gentlemen, it's the queen of the closet, DJ Blackbird," I say in an announcer's voice as I continue beatboxing.

Raven laughs as she says, "I may use that for my channel. Or...for the booth I will have at the OooLaLa! event downtown next month." The smile she gives me is more cat-that-caught-the-canary than blackbird.

"What?!" I exclaim, overjoyed at this news. "You got in? I mean, of course you did. You're fucking amazing, but you did it. I'm so thrilled for you. Congratulations."

"Thanks Liam. I'm pretty pumped."

"As well you should be. Can't believe it wasn't the first thing you said when you saw me tonight. Anyway, good for you. I hope I'll be able to come."

"You mean because you and Devontay have always wanted to go?" She teases.

"Because I want to be there to support you," I say earnestly.

"That would be lovely. So, how much do you charge for voiceover work?" She steers the conversation back to playful territory.

"Oh, my rates are very negotiable," I flirt, leaning over to steal a kiss from her inviting red lips.

“Until your career takes off,” she says as our lips part. “Then I won’t be able to afford you.”

“You kidding? By then I’m hoping you won’t be able to get rid of me,” I tell her perhaps a little too honestly.

“That sounds like it could be a pretty good problem to have,” she admits with a hint of coyness.

Our eyes lock and the need for words melts away. I lean in closer to her, compelled by her, to take her face in my hand and kiss her again.

But just as we’re a breath away from giving in to that shared energy, my phone breaks the mood, rudely ringing from my pocket. I pull it out to see my agent’s name across the screen.

“Shite, this is my agent,” I say. “I should take this.”

“Of course, you should take it, Liam. Put it on speaker, what if it’s about the movie?”

“What if it’s bad news?” I grumble.

“Agents don’t call with bad news,” she points out. “Then, they just don’t call.”

Thinking she makes a pretty good point and knowing I’m going to tell her what happened either way, I place the call on speaker, holding the phone between the two of us.

“Hey Molly, this is Liam,” I open in my lilting brogue. “What’s up?”

“Don’t you mean… Jett Lockhart?” She announces loudly into the receiver.

“What? Seriously?”

“Just got off the phone with Dennis. You blew them out of the water, babe. You’re hired. You’re it. You’re the guy. Congratulations.”

“Holy shit. That’s incredible,” I say, stunned. “I can’t believe it.”

“Well, believe it. Their team is putting the offer terms together, but we’ve agreed in principle since it’s such a short turnaround. I’m gonna get you paid; don’t you worry. For now, celebrate. Next week, you’re wheels up, baby.”

“Wow, ok. Right. This is all pretty hard to believe,” I tell her, the first hint of reality breaking through this euphoric moment.

"Well, believe it, Liam. This is happening. Congratulations, kid. More tomorrow."

We hang up the call and I stare at Raven, dumbfounded. She beams back. "Hello there, movie star," she purrs, then pulls me to her to plant a kiss on me.

"Hello to you too, fashion icon," I growl right back at her.

Still reeling from the past few moments, gobsmacked by the enormity of this news for both of us, Raven threads her long, thin fingers through mine as the lights dim and the movie begins.

Two hilarious hours later, Raven and I take in the picnic blanket carnage around us. An empty wine bottle, crushed seltzer cans, and an assortment of to-go containers speak to a wonderfully gluttonous evening. Reluctantly, I uncurl my hands from hers to begin tidying up. She offers me a quick kiss on my cheek as we separate which is playful, and definitely not friendly. I look over at her beaming face.

"That's quite a smile," I say, my own face mirroring hers.

"That was fun. This is fun."

"I completely agree. Feel like that movie gets better every time I watch it."

"No," she challenges with a professorial air. "It's because we're outside."

"Oh, really?"

"Yes. It's a scientific fact that comedies and horror films are best viewed outdoors."

"And here I thought the company had something to do with it."

"Or maybe the news that you just became a movie star?!"

"Yeah, this has been a wild night." A pause. "I don't want it to end."

"Neither do I," she coos. "Take me back to my place, Irish."

The power of her gaze, the fire in her eyes renders me speechless. "Ok," is the only word in the English language I can muster.

"And stay with me."

It's not a question, but I answer anyway. "Ok."

I don't know when or how it happened, but at this moment, sitting on this plaid blanket across from this blackbird, I am entranced. Framed in front of the starlit night, Raven glows. Her onyx hair hiding in the sky, her face a galaxy of its own. For a moment, as I take her in, it's impossible to tell where the night ends and she begins. They are one. A ceaseless constellation of wonder.

Lost in this infinite moment, lost in her, I become fundamentally aware of the meaninglessness of time. The uselessness of words. They hold no sway now. Not tonight.

With dozens of sated movie-goers milling about, the palm trees doing their lazy dance, we are alone in a sea of people. Her eyes, like the stars, sparkle with secrets. Taunting, inviting, alluring. Irresistible. And as the truth of all this hits me, one word escapes: "Raven."

Her name, unchained from the very core of me, says nothing. Says everything. And as our eyes hold each other, our bodies pull together in an orbit all their own, and there is nothing left to do but kiss her.

So, I do.

CHAPTER EIGHTEEN

I HAVE A TOOTHBRUSH AT RAVEN'S PLACE NOW.

After that otherworldly kiss, we left Hollywood Forever, stopping at a pharmacy on the way to her place to outfit me for an overnight. Deodorant, box of condoms, toothbrush: the budding relationship emergency kit. It only seemed fitting to celebrate this momentous occasion with sex. Lots of it. Which we did.

In the morning with diffused light filtering in past her curtains, I woke with Raven's warmth pressed snugly against me. In the past, I've not been much for physical contact while sleeping, but waking with my hand resting on her flat stomach, my index finger softly grazing the swell of her full breasts, I cannot imagine sleeping any other way again.

The newness of this relationship coupled with my impending travel for this film break me from that thought process, but I push those anxieties aside and focus on this moment. Burying my face in her hair, inhaling her citrus scent, I pepper the back of her neck with sucking kisses and teasing nibbles. My hand slides greedily north to take full hold of her glorious breasts. She rouses on a throaty cat-like rasp while grinding herself against my rigid length. We move in gentle waves together, no words needed. Her pert nipples, her guttural moans telling me she's right here with me.

I lean away long enough to grab another condom from the nightstand, then return my body to the warmth of our shared space. This time, as my hand slides around her hip to her stomach, I venture south, running my fingers up and down, caressing her wet slit.

While two fingers circle her clit, I pour into her from behind, her soft center hugging me in its own warmth. My blackbird takes flight, her body shaking in ecstasy after only a few luxurious thrusts. I lengthen my strokes as my hand travels the length of her body through the valley of her breasts to take hold of her throat.

My mouth finds her ear, sucking and kissing, as my arm presses her body tight against my chest. Her moans ratchet up as her hips take control, grinding and massaging my cock as I hold her upper body tight to mine. In a few dizzyingly short moments, Raven coaxes me to my release as my legs tighten and contract. My orgasm shoots through me, thrusting myself just that much deeper into her.

Our moans and sighs blend together until I'm finally able to form words. "Good morning," I rasp in her ear, somehow remembering to flavor my voice with a hint of Irish.

"Certainly fucking is," she replies on her next breath.

After a quick trip to the bathroom to clean up, I return with a washcloth for Raven. I check my phone. 10am and the emails about the movie are pouring in.

At the look on my face, Raven asks, "Everything ok?"

"Oh yeah, everything's fine. Just getting a ton of work texts and emails, looks like. I hate to do this, but.."

Before I can finish, Raven interjects. "Don't be silly. Go. This has been great."

"Maybe we could do lunch?" I offer, then remember the day. "No, shit. Sorry. I have a standing date with my niece. Tomorrow, maybe?"

"That sounds good. Just text me. We'll figure something out."

"That's very chill, thank you," I say, finishing up getting dressed. "Can I make you some coffee before I head out?"

"A man who knows the way to my heart."

"Caffeine? That easy, huh?"

"Morning sex and caffeine," she flirts. "In that order."

I laugh as I lean across the bed to give her one more kiss before heading into her kitchen to brew her a pot.

CHAPTER NINETEEN

"Hollywood King Maker Dennis Lawson looks to be molding a new crown for Irish newcomer Liam O'Connell. After an impressive debut turn on *Boise Patrol* (airing Thursday night) Dennis tapped the chisel-jawed stud for the lead opposite Hollywood icon, Abigail Summers, for his hotly-anticipated and expected blockbuster *Nowhere to Hide*. Pre-production is wrapped with filming scheduled to begin in Montana next week," my brother finishes reading, then looks up from his phone. We stand opposite each other at his kitchen island. I take a sip of water, shock and confusion plastered on Ryan's face. "This is nuts."

"I can't believe that's out already," I say, sharing my brother's feelings on the subject. "I just found out last night."

"This is *Variety,* dude. Like the front page of *Variety.* Like when you go to their website, this is the first thing you see. I'm staring at your face on the home page of the biggest industry trade publication. This is nuts."

"You said that already," I point out.

"Well, it bears repeating."

"Fair."

"What are you going to do?"

"What do you mean, 'what am I going to do'? I'm gonna go to Montana to shoot a film, bro," I say confidently, though if I'm being honest with myself, I'm starting to have serious doubts about myself. I was nobody before the accent. Maybe I'm still nobody without the accent. But that's a problem for another day at this point. I continue filling Ryan in on the details. "I've been getting emails and phone calls about this all day. I leave Sunday. Script was already delivered. I'm in, like, all the scenes."

"I can't believe this is happening this fast."

"Well, I wouldn't say super-fast. Took eight years to get to this point. It's only going fast now."

"Pretty fast since you concocted this insane Irish persona ruse," Ryan argues.

"Listen. It's still me. Just because he's got a different name doesn't mean I'm not the one doing the work. Creating the product. If anything, the fake name gives me a sense of invincibility. Like a mask I can hide behind to be a more fearless version of myself. Does that make sense?" And I'm not sure who I'm trying to convince more with that explanation, Ryan or myself.

"I'd say very little of this makes sense right now, Will."

"Oh, and in my defense, your wife concocted this insane ruse, not me. Speaking of which, I need to get her a super nice gift. What does Hazel like?"

"Spa days, handbags, and Swiss chocolates," he rattles off rapid-fire from years of experience. "Have you got an endgame here?"

"Endgame? Ryan, this whole thing just started. For now, I keep it going, obviously. I figure if I can get this film shot and it goes well, then I can use the momentum of that good press to come clean and build a more authentic brand from there." Ryan looks on skeptically, so I continue. "Look, I nailed the audition. Will did that. I earned the role. Will did that too. The work speaks for itself."

"Yeah, but it's currently speaking for itself with a thick Irish brogue."

"It's really more of an understated Dubliner vibe, but I hear you," I retort. "Will did the work, but Liam's getting the credit. But it's all me at the end of the day. You said yourself, nobody cares who you are until you're somebody. If Liam sells, who is Will to deny him?"

"Will," he begins, emphasizing the word aggressively, "you stop referencing your *selves* in the third person?"

"I *will* work on that," I respond with the same emphasis.

Ryan looks at his watch, then up at me, the time forcing an end to this conversation. "Ok, if you're picking up Lex, you need to leave now. You can take the Range Rover."

"Sweet," I say as Ryan tosses me the keys. I head out to pick my niece up from school for our Wednesday afternoon date.

A little while later, Lexi eyes me as I take another bite of my salad.

"Why do you get that salad every time we come, Uncle Will?" she asks, plopping her napkin down on an empty plate of spaghetti.

"I told you, Bean. La Scala knows that the secret to a great salad is all about how finely you chop the lettuce. The smaller the lettuce, the tastier the salad. I don't have this much time for chopping lettuce. I leave that to the professionals."

"But they have other things on the menu," Lexi counters.

"Yeah, and none of them are as good as this salad. It's not like I'm eating this salad every day. That would be weird. I just eat it every time I come here which is only like once a month. You eat plenty of food more than once a month," I reason.

"Salads are gross," she retorts with confidence.

"Wrong. Salads are like boundless sandwiches unconstrained by the rigid confines of bread."

"Spaghetti is awesomer," she concludes, and I can tell when I'm bested.

"You got me there, sprout. Glad you liked it."

An idea comes to life on her face. "After lunch can we do window display stories, Uncle Will?"

I laugh, thinking about our invented game. "Absolutely, Lexi Bean. Let's get that check so we can motor."

Once outside, I wrap my arm around Lexi's shoulder while throwing on a pair of sunglasses to combat the midday sun. "Come on Lexi Bean, the world awaits."

"Why do you call me Bean?" She asks abruptly.

"I don't know, it's just a nickname I gave you."

"Yeah, but it had to have come from somewhere, Uncle Will."

"Well, I suppose, I thought you looked like a little bean when you were born. You were a few weeks early, so you were super tiny. And so, I've always called you my little bean."

"But I'm not little anymore. I think I should have a different nickname."

I consider her request, but answer seriously, "That's not how nicknames work, LB. You don't get to choose your own."

"Tell your own story, it's the one you know the best. That's what Mommy says," Lexi intones in a spot-on impression of her mother, crisp British accent and all.

I laugh at her performance, but do love the sentiment, so I say, "Ok, fair enough. I like that. So, what should it be?"

Lexi stops dead in her tracks in the middle of Rodeo Drive, her thinking so intense there can be no distractions, no other action like walking or talking. Pure focus. After several heady moments, she speaks.

"Well, once you plant a bean in the ground and it breaks through the earth, then it's called a sprout, right?"

"Yeah, that's definitely what that's called."

"That's me now." You can hear the smile in her voice.

"Lexi Sprout?" I repeat slowly, almost feeling the words in my mouth like a fine wine. "It's perfect," I emphatically insist. Then go on in a pompous, royal British accent. "Ok, take a knee my liege."

I pull a pretend sword from my belt and proceed to knight Lexi in the middle of the street. "Henceforth and evermore, Lexi Bean shall be known as Lexi Sprout, the duchess of Southern California."

Lexi giggles and stands. Gives me a big hug. And we continue our post-lunch trek in search of fun mannequin window displays to turn into fake storytelling adventures.

Lexi picks up from our earlier conversation about my new job. "Can't believe you're going to be in a whole movie."

"Me neither. Pretty wild."

A thought dawns on Lexi's face and she frowns. "Does this mean you'll miss my birthday party?"

"Absolutely not. I already told my agent that date was non-negotiable."

Lexi side tackles my leg, giving me a big squeeze.

"What about this one?" She asks as we approach the front of the Ralph Lauren store.

"Yeah, perfect. Ok, I'll be this guy with the plaid jacket pointing and you be the woman reclining over there with the thick glasses on. Cool?"

Lexi does not miss a beat and at once breaks into the scene. "I wish that waiter would come back with our cheese plate. I'm starving, Mortimer."

"Mortimer?" I giggle, totally breaking character already. Lexi stares me down reproachfully. "Yes, Bunny. It's been such a long day of lounging around in all this mismatched plaid. I'm sure he'll be here soon."

"I guess I'll just have another Shirley Temple while I'm waiting," Lexi chimes in as Bunny.

"Oh look, there he is now," I say in my stuffiest voice as we both dissolve into giggles.

Wrapping my arm around Lexi's shoulder, we turn back toward the street, still in the throes of laughter. We make it a few more steps before I'm stopped dead in my tracks by the pale-skinned pixie standing in front of us. Bags clutched in both her hands, the doe-eyed siren from last night (and this morning) stares directly at me.

"Raven," I say, forgetting my accent and losing all my composure. My heart rate instantly skyrockets as I try to take control of this situation. "What brings you west of La Cienega?" I say as calmly as I can, brogue firmly back in place.

"Shopping day for the show. Have to put together some looks for a few upcoming guest stars," she says, showing off the bags in both her hands.

"I had no idea the residents of Boise, Idaho had such good taste," I joke as Lexi squirms next to me.

"Dennis is directing this week, actually. Don't know when that man sleeps."

"He does seem to have a lot of energy," I reply.

"And who's this little one?" Raven asks looking down to my right at the poor innocent that's been thrust in the crosshairs of my deception, and I can only hope she has the smarts to play along.

I squeeze Lexi to me, pinching her shoulder as I talk, hoping she remembers my speaking about Raven and the Irish persona that's shaded a small part of my personality with her. "This is Lexi. My brother's daughter. My niece. Which of course is what the daughter of my brother is called. A niece. I'm sure you knew that. Everyone knows that. Unless of course, you forget if it's a niece or a nephew for a boy or a girl. And honestly, why do we have two words for that anyway? We should just use one word for any child of a sibling. Like Niece-phew. And their parents can just be Ancles. We insert gender into too much of our language, I say." Taking a deep breath, trying desperately to calm my rambling mouth, I wrap up this long-winded introduction. "Anyway, Raven, Lexi. Lexi, this is Raven, the incredible woman I'm seeing."

"Hi, Raven, nice to meet you," Lexi says with a smile. My stomach feels like it's halfway through the wash cycle as Lexi continues talking, just waiting for my entire ruse to go up in flames in front of the one person I wish more than anything I wasn't lying to. "Not sure if my Uncle Liam told you," and Lexi places just a slight emphasis on the word Liam as she looks up at me as if to say, don't worry Uncle, I've got this. "But I'm actually already six years old and the third tallest person in my class, so I'm really not little anymore. My childhood is behind me."

Raven laughs as she apologizes, "I did not mean to offend. You certainly seem like a delightful young lady. I'm sure your best days are still in front of you."

"You too," Lexi replies instantly. Then another thought materializes. It is incredible to watch ideas emerge in real-time on young faces. Nothing hidden, all just fearlessly exposed. "You should come to my birthday party in a couple weeks. I'm sure Liam mentioned it."

"I'm not sure if he has," Raven says looking my way. "But I'd love to be there."

"It's a Dragons and Dinosaurs party. We're going shopping for my outfit this weekend. I'm gonna be the fiercest dragon ever."

"You know, Lexi, Raven here is a costume designer," I interject, feeling comfortable that my mask is safe for now, thanks to Lexi's quick thinking. "She might know a great place to get an outfit."

Raven lights up at the idea. "I'll do you one better. How about I make you a costume?"

Lexi is floored. "What, really? That would be amazing."

"Oh, wow, Rave. You don't need to do that," I say. "That's a lot." And if I didn't already have serious feelings developing for this woman… I leave that thought hanging for now. Too much to unpack at the moment.

"Don't be silly. You kidding me? Dragon queen birthday party costume? I wish that was the only thing I ever made!"

"This is so cool," Lexi shouts, getting right down to business. "My favorite colors are purple and orange and I love sparkles and dragons that breathe magic." She says the last word with a special amount of reverence.

"Sounds like an extremely awesome dragon," Raven says, and I can't help but enjoy her sincerity and playfulness with my niece. "Liam, when you two get home, have her mom take a few measurements and send those along with her shirt, pants, and dress sizes right now. I can take it from there. When's the party?"

"Three weeks from Saturday," Lexi announces proudly.

"Great. This guy I really like is going to be out of town for a bit, so that will give me something fun to do while he's away," she whispers to Lexi while side-eyeing me.

Lexi giggles and looks my way. "She's talking about you."

"Shh, that was between us," Raven feigns with shock.

"Uncle, I like her. Please don't screw this up," Lexi deadpans.

"I will do my best, Lexi Sprout. I really will."

Birthday plans in place and the Will/Liam crisis averted for now, we say our goodbyes to Raven and head back to the car. Not only did Lexi not blow my cover, but she also managed to pull that blackbird in even further to me and the ones I love.

On the way home, I stop by Edelweiss for some of the best chocolate in the city to make good on my promise to get something nice for Hazel. I don't hesitate to get a trio of truffles for Lexi Sprout, too. I'm quite sure she's earned it.

CHAPTER TWENTY

Waking up Thursday morning, I am quite simply a ball of nerves. I decide on an impromptu morning paddle board session to even me out. Tonight is a big night. After eight years of hustle and almost a decade of rejection, tonight I make my television debut. I try to find some inner harmony through some outer balance work, but I'm spending more time in the Pacific than I am on my board today. One source of calm keeps flying through my thoughts: Raven. Last night, I'd sent Lexi's measurements over to her via text and we proceeded to chat all night. Emojis, GIFs, dragon costume Pinterest boards… we covered it all with our thumbs. And I loved every stinking second of it. But as quickly as those memories fill me up, the anxiety about seeing myself on TV returns, and off the board I fall. I paddle back to shore resigned to the fact that calm just won't be a prevalent mood today. Only so much I can control.

That evening, Von picks me up to take me over to my brother's place for a special screening of my episode. I'm touched that Ryan and Hazel want to make a big deal out of this, but we were going to come over regardless since

Ryan's the only person I know who still has actual cable anymore. When Devontay and I pull up to my brother's place, black and gold balloons hang from the front gate and, not going to lie, pull on my heart strings. Feels good to have people who want to celebrate my wins with me. The gate hangs ajar and when we walk through, they've laid a red carpet out leading to the entrance to their house with more swaying balloons inviting us in.

"Your family loves you, man," Devontay says sincerely with a firm squeeze of my shoulder.

Words fail me in the moment, so I pat Von on the back and we walk up the steps.

"There he is, the man of the hour," Hazel announces lyrically as we walk in.

"Uncle Will!" Lexi exclaims, barreling into me. "I'm so excited you're going to be on TV tonight."

"I'm excited too, Lexi Sprout."

"It means I get to stay up past my bedtime," she confesses in full voice.

"And there it is. Truth hurts, bud," Von laughs as he makes his way to the kitchen island to greet Ryan and Hazel. He's got his eyes on the generous food spread laid out too.

"You guys. This is a lot," I say taking it all in. "You didn't need to do all this. It's just a couple scenes on a show."

"This is your television debut, little brother. Of course, we had to do this," Ryan puts in.

Hazel pops the top on a bottle of Sparkling Apple Cider and passes glasses around to all of us.

"To the first of many," Hazel toasts with her arm raised.

We all clink glasses and repeat her refrain.

"Now dig in, everyone. I tried to do an Idaho theme for the food, but honestly, there were only so many things I could do with potatoes," Hazel says indicating the plates on the counter. "So French fries, chicken tenders, and Caprese salad will have to do."

"I'm sure they have basil in Boise," Von says, helping himself to a huge plate.

"Ranch dressing on a ranch works too," Lexi chimes in. "See, you did great, Mom."

Ryan checks his watch. "Five minutes, people. Load up and get moving."

Everyone grabs a plate and helps themselves, then we migrate over to the living room to grab spots on the couch.

"Is Raven not coming?" Lexi asks as I take my seat.

"She is currently filming another episode of this very show and tonight is running long, so no Sprout. I'm afraid she couldn't make it."

"Dodged a bullet there, leprechaun," Von mumbles, emphasizing the 'con' on the end of the word. I don't know how he keeps coming up with these ridiculous puns, but he's not wrong. I'm not sure what I would have done if Raven had been able to join us tonight. I know I want her here. That feeling is all too clear. But before I can chase that line of thought too far down the rabbit hole, Hazel grabs the remote and turns the volume up as the show's grave narration intro fills the room.

"'In a city known for outlaws, it takes a special kind of officer to keep the peace. When the stakes are this high, not just any police force will do. Idaho relies on a dedicated team to ensure its streets are safe. This is Boise Patrol."

"Guest-starring Liam O'Connell! There he is people." My brother exclaims as my name pops up on the lower third during the opening credits and everyone in the room applauds.

A surge of pride jolts through me. If the thrill of seeing my name on a film trailer was exhilarating, the feeling of reading my name in 4k clarity on a big-screen TV is otherworldly. As the living room lights dim, we all grab places on the couch and turn our attention to the show, while I think to myself maybe this crazy scheme might be worth it after all.

One hour later, the room erupts in another chorus of cheers as the end credits roll. "Liam O'Connell as Clint Rogers. It's official. We've got a working actor in the room, everybody," Devontay booms as Hazel brings the lights up in the living room.

"Wow," I say, taking all of it in.

"Wow is right, Uncle Will," Lexi yawns. "You shouldn't have devoted your life to crime. You got what you deserved," she says of my character's eventual jail sentencing.

"And let that be a lesson to you, little one," Ryan says, ruffling Lexi's hair.

"Now, pajamas and brush your teeth, young lady," Hazel commands, her accent giving off serious Mary Poppins vibes when she gives Lexi instructions.

Lexi hangs her head but immediately moves toward her room. She stops by me on her way out to offer more encouragement. "Great job. It's clear to me you have that unteachable charisma that Hollywood is always looking for. This is only the beginning, Uncle Will."

"She's not wrong," Hazel chimes in as I sit there slack-jawed by this six-year-old's compliment. "Precocious, but not wrong."

"Thanks, you guys," I tell the room as Lexi heads off. "You made this night real special, and it means a lot to me. Also, pretty sure all this madness is partially your fault Hazel, so I'm excited to share it with you."

As I say these words, my mind immediately jumps to thoughts of the other person I wish was in this room. That onyx-haired siren has taken up permanent residence in my mind. And I am totally fine with that. I glance around at all the people who mean something to me in this city. And as wonderful as all these people are, it feels somehow incomplete.

The path forward materializes clearly in my mind. I want Raven. I trust Raven. And in order for our relationship to work, she needs to trust me too. That can only begin when I come clean to her. Let her in to all of me, the real William. With my plan forming in my head, I reach for my phone to text Raven, only to see one I missed from her already.

> **Raven:** Hope the premiere went well. I'm sure you were phenomenal, Clint. Wish I could have been there.

> **Me:** Just got your message. The show was awesome. You were definitely missed.

She shoots back a heart emoji, the red kind, and my fingers fly over the keyboard, my pulse pounding.

Me: Clear your calendar this weekend. Don't say no.

She does not leave me waiting long.

Raven: I'm all yours.

My body buzzes as I read those words. I quickly open a different app on my phone and hastily make a hotel reservation. Once that's done, my focus comes back to the room. Three sets of expectant eyes staring at me, wondering what I'm doing.

"You ok, man?" Devontay asks. "You look a little possessed."

I don't have time to answer him. Instead, I turn my attention directly to my brother. "Ryan, I need to borrow the Range Rover."

CHAPTER TWENTY-ONE

RAVEN GOT TO SET FIRST THING FRIDAY MORNING TO PULL OUTFITS for that day's filming, in hopes that Carlotta would let her go early. Apparently, there was also a new trainee on hand, so Carlotta was fine with releasing Rave at lunch so we could beat the afternoon traffic out of the city.

It still took us an hour to get past Malibu because there is never not traffic in Los Angeles, but if you're gonna crawl down the highway, doing it with a beautiful woman on your right and the Pacific Ocean on your left is the way to go.

The traffic opens up past Zuma beach. Raven cranks the windows down and turns the Sublime up. We cruise up the coast, *Santeria* blaring and the wind whipping through the car, turning inland near Santa Barbara until we find our way to one of the most charming little towns in all of America: Solvang. Nicer than anything around Cincinnati anyway. (Sorry Covington).

Once we check into our room and set our bags down, Raven comments on how surreal that drive was for her. "We're like halfway to my house from here." There's something a touch ominous about the way she says it.

"Really?"

"Well, it's probably closer to another three hours to Fresno. Bakersfield would be the real halfway point from LA, but…"

"Who wants to go to Bakersfield?" We finish together.

I check my watch, then suggest a plan. "Unless you're super hungry, I thought we could walk around downtown a little bit? Check out a few shops, then there's this awesome Biergarten that I thought would be a perfect landing spot for some drinks and dinner. What do you think?"

"Every building we passed on the way in looked like a magical fairy tale cottage, so yes Liam. All I want to do is walk around pretending to be Hansel and Gretel all day."

"Maybe we should eat first then. Don't want to get lured away by any witches."

We both laugh and I wrap my arm firmly around Raven's trim waist and pull her up to me to kiss her lips. One taste has me second-guessing our afternoon plans, which I imagine is evident to Raven as my pants bulge against her thigh.

She looks down at my crotch with a smirk. "Come on, big guy. I want to see as much of this fairy tale village as we can before the sun sets."

If I'm not going to get an afternoon bj, then walking hand in hand with this lithe siren along Solvang's adorable, cobblestone streets is a reasonable consolation prize. We spend the next two hours popping in and out of shops, sharing a flaky, warm raspberry Danish from Olsen's, and making out whenever I can convince Raven to stop walking.

As the sun begins to set, painting the facades of these thatch-roofed storefronts in shades of pink and purple, our stomachs lead us directly to the Copenhagen Sausage Garden right in the middle of downtown.

We grab a table for two, order several brats to share, and two giant steins of lager. When the frothy mugs are planted firmly on our table, we laugh at their ridiculous size, toast, and take a sip. This has been a perfect afternoon, but my mind loops back around to the reason that we are here.

Showing Raven the time of her life before I leave for the month is obviously important, but coming clean to her is critical. The gentle hum of other conversations washes over us and though we're in a crowd, it feels like it always does when I'm with Raven. Like we are the only two people in the world.

"This afternoon has been incredible, Blackbird," I tell Raven, and her brown eyes shimmer when she hears that nickname.

"One might even say magical. I can't believe I grew up three hours from this place and never knew it existed."

"Hey, the only reason I've been is because my brother and Hazel brought me along last year to chaperone Lexi while they drank all of the wine for their anniversary."

"That sounds like a pretty awesome weekend, Liam."

"Not as great as this one," I rumble. Then I take a deep breath to steel myself for this conversation. Just as I'm about to dive in, we are interrupted by a tenor voice approaching our table.

"Ray, is that you?" A tall blond guy with a forest for a beard and mountains for shoulders asks.

The look on Raven's face is one I have not seen before. Shock only describes part of it. "Brett, oh. Wow. What are you doing here?"

"I'm down here for a wedding. I'd ask you the same question," he says insinuating something. What? I wish I knew.

Everything about this scene has my hair standing on end—the look of this dude, the sound of her voice. The history here between these two is undeniable. What the pages of that chapter in her life entail, I have no idea. Maybe they're still being written.

I decide to make my presence known. "Thought I'd take my girlfriend out for a romantic weekend. Beautiful drive up the coast with my bird, room service, cold beers. I'm Liam, by the way," I say, unleashing my secret weapon straight out of the gate, a lyrical accent with plenty of bass.

I don't even have time to relish the fact that I just called Raven my girlfriend for the first time or how easily it rolled off the tongue. Felt so right. Because this guy eyes me warily, seeming to enjoy his vantage point from above since he's standing and we are sitting. He's also impossibly tall, the bastard. If it wouldn't come off as too aggressive, I'd gladly stand right now. If for no other reason than to see how tall he really is compared to me. He seems to pick up on my energy as he throws a smirk our way, then glares one more time at Raven. The tension is broken by a guy in a plaid button-down yelling in our direction. "Brett, you coming? Party's moving to the next spot."

Blond Brett downs the rest of his blond beer in one long pull, then yells over his shoulder, "On my way, Derek." He returns his attention to Raven. "It was great to see you, Ray. Let me know if you're ever back up in Fresno."

"Yeah, ok, Brett. I'll be sure to do that."

With one last leer, Brett makes his way across the crowded patio leaving me trying to unpack Raven's distinct change in mood.

"Are you ok?"

"I'm fine," she dismisses. Then after a deep sigh, she continues. "That was my ex."

Her ex the freaking Adonis. And he did not seem to be looking at her like he had moved on. If Raven found out she'd left that live-action superhero for me—a Midwest nobody whose agent didn't even remember the sound of my voice—She'd be back in Fresno before I could say 'Erin Go Bragh'. Who am I kidding? Raven isn't into Will, it's Liam the Irish TV star that's winning her over. I can feel my courage evaporate.

And yet, she seems visibly shaken, so I forget my worries and extend my hand across the table to clasp hers.

"We don't have to talk about him," I tell her. "Honestly, we shouldn't talk at all if we are ever planning on finishing these gigantic beers. Who drinks this much at a time?"

The laugh helps break some of the tension, but resolve replaces the worry on my Blackbird's face as she speaks. "You're right. Bottoms up, Irish."

And in one swift motion, Raven sets about dousing that fire in her eyes by downing the remaining contents of her stein. Briefly, I wonder what Raven's leaving unsaid. My concerned thoughts turn carnal as I watch her thin throat bob with each successive pull from her beer. Before my reeling mind can head off on any more tangents, she slams her stein with an authoritative and somehow-still-sexy belch.

"Well, that was something," I say, dumbfounded.

"This is supposed to be a celebratory weekend… So, let's celebrate." She flags the waitress down, ordering two more beers and a couple of Jägermeister shots.

"Suppose I better polish this one off, then," I say, not totally upset at the new direction our night seems to be taking, though I am still concerned about her being upset. "You sure you're ok?"

Raven softens slightly as her initial reaction to that last encounter settles in and she gets some control over the moment. For the first time since I've known her, my porcelain princess looks breakable, and it nearly breaks me right along with her. Her almond eyes glaze over as her hand takes mine across the table. "Sorry. That was a lot. But right now, I don't want to think about my past. I want to be enjoying this present with you."

That declaration goes some way to easing my anxiety about her well-being as one of the cornier things I've ever said to Raven slips past my lips. "And what a present it is, Blackbird."

A smirk plays on her face at that silly line as the waitress returns with our ambitiously ordered round. Raven eyes the dark liquor with trepidation. "These might have been a poor decision."

"Hey, like you said, this is a celebration," I say, offering her a glass and then raising mine to hers. We toast silently, our locked eyes speaking volumes. We both do our best to hide our winces as we chase the syrupy shot with some cold beer.

"That definitely tasted better when I was in college."

"Would have to agree. Jag definitely does not age well."

"Sorry," she says with a shiver.

"No apology necessary. Now, do I need to go find this Brett character and kick his arse?" As I speak, I pull the hoodie off my back in one smooth motion, reaching over the small table to lay the cotton across Raven's delicate shoulders.

She smiles at the gesture, more of the tension leaving her as she shifts the mood back to more playful territory as I re-take my seat. "No, Mr.

Soon-To-Be-Movie-Star," the nickname inadvertently rubbing me the wrong way. "In fact, I don't want you thinking about his ass at all."

I let flirtation dominate doubt. "Oh, is there, by chance, a different ass, I should have occupying my mind?"

"As a matter of fact, there is," she rasps playfully.

"And would that ass happen to want to go back to the hotel room with me?"

"As a matter of fact, it would."

"That sounds great to me. As long as you're fine abandoning these gigantic beers."

"We did just order these, didn't we?"

"You did, yes. In a fit of ex-boyfriend rage."

"We'd never finish these anyway, would we?" She asks coyly, eyeing down the mega big gulp amount of beer in front of her.

"I'd much rather drink you in all night, anyway," I rasp lyrically.

Decidedly done talking, Raven stands, clutching my sweatshirt to herself, while twisting out of her seat to give me a deliciously teasing look at that beautifully sculpted backside. I fumble for some cash which I lay on the table, eyes glancing away from her only briefly.

Raven does not turn around. Just saunters confidently toward the exit, like Orpheus with courage.

Knowing, quite rightly, that I am only too glad to follow.

CHAPTER TWENTY-TWO

THE NEXT MORNING MY EYES FLUTTER OPEN AND THE WORLD SLOWLY slips into focus. The warmth radiating against my left side generated by the blackbird breathing softly against me manages to heat my whole body. With the curtains drawn, I cannot tell what time it is, but once again I find myself disinterested in its passage when I'm with Raven. My only thought about time that I wish it would simply freeze; stand still, so we can spend more of it together.

Memories of last night pour into my foggy head. Running into Raven's ex sent our evening spiraling down a detour, uncharted territory we had to navigate in real-time. That navigation took us back to this hotel room for an aggressive round of sex followed by an even more aggressive round of cuddling. And now, here we are, lying together. Both of us now, it would seem, with some truths left unsaid.

Last night might have been the first time I've seen Raven guarded. I have been so fixated on my own secrets, it never occurred to me to wonder about hers. But her truths are hers to reveal to me when she's ready. I planned this trip spontaneously to spend time with this woman who's monopolizing more of my thoughts with each passing day before I head off to film for three weeks. But I also know if we stand a chance in the long run, I need to come clean and trust her to understand why I've adopted the Liam persona and let her know the real me.

I try to ignore my misgivings about Viking Brett and screw my courage to the sticking place. Resolved to maintain my course and see out this plan, I let my eyes drift closed, enjoying these still moments with a sleeping Raven.

Sometime later, we both wake up and agree that showers are in order to wash away the dregs of last night. Once clean and checked out of our hotel room, we stop in town for some hot coffee and warm pastries. Then it's back in my brother's roomy Range Rover for a short drive down some lush, winding, grape-dappled roads which eventually deposit us not at one of the area's many vineyards, but rather at one of the area's more unique attractions: Ostrichland.

"Where are we?" Raven asks as I pull us into the parking lot.

"I would have thought the name on the sign kind of gave it away, but if it wasn't quite clear, Rave, we have indeed arrived in a land of ostriches. Allow me to take you on a brief tour to gaze on the majesty of one of the world's only flightless birds."

At Raven's skeptical expression, I continue the pitch. "On TripAdvisor, Daphne from Glendora said this place was whimsical and not to be missed."

"Why didn't you open with that?" Raven smiles, her sarcasm both fun and flirtatious. "If I'd known Daphne from Glendora had spoken so fondly, I'd already have jumped out of the car."

As we then exit and round the front of the car, I take Raven in a side hug, pulling her against me and burying my face in her jet-black hair. A vanilla aroma richer than any bean in Madagascar assaults my nostrils and I plant a kiss in her hair. Intoxicated by this blackbird.

We walk the grounds in lock step, neither of us seeming to want to break the physical connection. There's honestly not that much to Ostrichland, just dozens of long-necked birds fighting aggressively to pluck birdseed from giggling visitors. But it occurs to me at that moment, that it wouldn't matter what we were doing, as long as I'm doing it with Raven. That thought firmly in the front of my mind, I decide there is no time like the present. As Raven extends her full-fisted hand to feed a gaggle of these pecking monsters, I blurt out, "Rave, I need to tell you something." Just moments away from dropping my accent and leaving the truth laid out between us, Raven turns her head back toward me at the earnestness in my voice. Just as I'm about to continue, my blackbird lets out an unholy scream. Both of us look immediately at her hand which has just been mercilessly stabbed by one of these gangly-necked feather demons. The pellets of food have been replaced by drops of blood pooling in her palm.

"Holy shit, Rave. Are you ok?" Fear for her wellbeing overtakes my composure causing me to lose my accent momentarily and reach for the first thing I can think of to stop the bleeding, which in this case, is my white t-shirt, which I pull off over my head. She doesn't seem to notice the vocal slip, too focused on the pain. I slip the accent back on as I wrap the shirt around her hand. "Let's get you to the office. I'm sure they've got a first aid kit."

The usually pale Raven has blanched a bleach white. "My hands are my livelihood, Liam. What if something happened? I've got my show coming up."

Staring directly into her eyes, listening to her fear and vulnerability, I am overcome by a need to protect her. Not protect her, that's not quite right, as Raven has shown me time and again she's more than capable of taking care of herself. But keep her safe, even when I know I can't. Because her happiness brightens my world now. I derive joy from her joy. And right now, she's in pain and I need to do what I can to help.

"You pulled your hand back right away, I'm sure it's just a nick. Keep it elevated," I say, as I slide my hand to her wrist and guide the arm above her heart as my other hand steers her back toward the main office.

The oafish man behind the counter inside seems decidedly less anxious about this situation than we are. "You're not supposed to feed them directly from your hand. That's why we have the plastic bowls," he drones on in a voice that indicates this isn't the first time this has happened.

"Thanks, but right now, we don't need a lecture on proper bird feeding techniques. We need a sink, some hydrogen peroxide, and some gauze." My tone brooks no argument, and he immediately hands off a kit he keeps stored beneath the desk. "Bathroom is the door on the right opposite the postcard rack."

Once inside the bathroom, I pour some warm running water over Raven's hand, trying to assess the damage while simultaneously calming her down. The cut looks superficial, and the bleeding has slowed noticeably already.

"It looks good, Rave. Can you wiggle your fingers?"

"I think so," she offers as she does as I ask.

"Great. And your wrist. Any pain? Can you rotate it?"

I guide her through some range of motion exercises which she handles with no noticeable pain response. After applying some hydrogen peroxide to the wound then dabbing it dry, I ask if she can make a fist.

She opens and closes her hand several times, then relaxes as I gently wrap gauze around her wrist and palm.

As I finish the wrap, I gently take her hand in mine, locking eyes with my softly shaking siren. "It looks good, Rave. Just a nick. And no damage to the muscles, tendons, or bone. You should be fine once that abrasion scabs over."

She relaxes visibly as her breathing evens out. "Thank you, Liam. How did you know how to do all that?"

"I played sports growing up. I know my way around a med kit."

"Well, I am super grateful. And not gonna lie, pretty freakin' turned on right now too. Ripping the shirt off was an especially nice touch."

I laugh as I say, "Sorry. I panicked. Saw blood, wanted to stop it."

"Do not apologize. I'm sorry my blood ruined your shirt," she talks over me, bringing her good hand to rest between my pecs. "You're my hero," she rasps, closing the distance between us. "I'm going to kiss you now."

And kiss we do. Better than any movie moment. An embrace full of tenderness, passion, and longing. After an amount of time I can only describe as 'not long enough', Raven looks up into my eyes, whispering, "Now, let me go buy you a souvenir t-shirt."

Twenty minutes later, we are making our way down the coast. Me, sporting a brand-new powder blue Ostrichland T-shirt, while Raven sits curled up in the passenger seat next to me. Once my mind had had a chance to clear from that traumatic event, I did not feel deterred, hoping to still have a chance to talk with Raven on the drive back to the city. But before we even reached the Pacific Coast Highway, my blackbird has closed her eyes, seeking quiet and rest after that harrowing incident. And I don't blame her. And I'm certainly not going to bother her.

I spend the next two hours blissfully driving down the coast stealing glances at this goddess resting next to me. The light pouring in paints the contrast between her fair skin and dark hair in sharp relief. She radiates like a figure in a Caravaggio painting.

Another thought follows fast on the heels of that one. The realization that this is all I've ever wanted. Raven is all I have ever wanted. I want her falling asleep on road trips next to me. I want her falling asleep on the couch next to me. I want her falling asleep in bed next to me. I want her… Next to me.

Lost in that blissed-out daze, the next thing I know I'm pulling off the 101 to drop Raven off before heading to my place to pack before a car picks me up for the airport.

Double-parked outside her place, I touch her arm gently. "We're here, Blackbird."

She mumbles softly as she slowly wakes up, and somehow that noise is even cuter than the vision of her sleeping.

"We're back already?"

"Well, you've been sleeping for about two hours, but yes, we're home. You're home."

"And you're leaving me," she pouts as reality comes crashing in.

"Yes, I am. I actually need to get going, I'm afraid. A car is coming to get me in a couple hours."

"A car? Well, look at you," she pokes me playfully in the ribs.

"I know. It's pretty ridiculous."

"No, Liam. I'm kidding," Raven instantly sobers. "It's awesome. You're awesome. Congratulations. Go kill it. I'm really proud of you."

"Thanks, Raven. That means a lot to me."

Then just as we're about to part ways, a thought slams into her and she exclaims, "Oh! You were about to say something. Before the malicious attack."

"No, it's nothing. I'm just glad you're ok," I deflect.

"Come on, you can tell me anything. You seemed very focused."

This is it. My last chance to come clean before heading off to shoot this film. And I am swimming in a sea of doubt. What if she's thinking about Brett? What if she's only attracted to my accent? And I'm not sure if it's the fear of losing her; the concern that I don't have enough time right now to set things in order; but the truth does not come out. Well, that truth doesn't. Though another one does. Looking at Raven, that sea of doubt is replaced by a flood of memories. From our heartfelt conversations to our incendiary physical connection, a feeling so honest, so pure, and so intense forces its way out of me. A truth so new, so raw, that it takes us both by surprise when I tell her, unequivocally, "I love you, Raven."

For the second time today, Raven pales. And though that was not the truth I meant to reveal, the second I hear the words out loud, I know them to be the truest I've ever spoken. The moment those words float between us, I feel grounded. Connected. Like the fluttery feeling I have every time I'm around Raven becomes weighted. Like an anvil untethered by gravity. Solid, and simultaneously weightless.

Before I realize that I've voiced none of those thoughts and am merely lost in my own head, Raven's words bring me back. "No, you don't Liam. That's way too fast. You're just saying that because you're about to leave."

"No, I'm saying that because it's true. It's a coincidence that I'm leaving. And I wanted you to know that before I left. You don't need to say it back to me. I'm not expecting it, honestly. And we can still take our time with this. Before I get on that plane, I just wanted you to know. That's all."

A silence descends. I don't want to call it awkward, but I imagine that Raven might.

"I don't need to hear you say it, Rave. I swear. Can we just leave it there for now? A joyous, positive thing. That's all it needs to be. A seed. And now that we know it's there, we can help it grow."

"Ok, Liam. That works for me. I *really* don't want you to fucking leave now though, you idiot."

"That's fair. I hadn't thought of that. I swear though, time will fly by. We can text and FaceTime and before you know it, I'll be back for your show."

"And Lexi's birthday," she reminds me. "I can't wait to be your date," Raven purrs, inches from my mouth.

Oh, God, the birthday. Meeting my family. Something I desperately want for our relationship, but she'll know the minute Ryan opens his Midwest mouth that I'm a fraud. I absolutely have to tell her before then. But I can't drop that bomb right now and then just leave. And, selfish as it might be, I have to be Liam for this movie.

"You're going to be the sexiest Brontosaurus in pre-history," I hum instead, wrapping her tight against me, pouring myself into her with one final kiss.

CHAPTER TWENTY-THREE

"ON BEHALF OF MAJESTIC AIRLINES, ALLOW ME TO BE THE FIRST to welcome you to Billings, Montana. We hope you enjoy your stay here or wherever your final destination may take you. We know you have a choice when flying, and we thank you for choosing to Fly Majestic." The bubbly flight attendant croons into the intercom as our plane taxis to its gate. I'm the first person off the plane because they booked me in first freakin' class. I honestly had no idea that air travel could be a pleasant experience. I am now officially ruined for coach. Better hope this career keeps taking off because I have seen behind the front row curtain, tasted of its warmed cookies, and drank of its flavored seltzers served in real glass champagne flutes… and I do not want to go back. Ever.

Backpack slung over one shoulder, I saunter into the terminal and head for baggage claim. My phone pings with an email from Lenny Schneider with next month's invoice for class. I've got too much on my mind right now to reply, plus I obviously won't be in class this month, so I ignore it, thinking I'll explain and pay him later. The second I pass by the security threshold, a portly man in a smart-looking black suit holds an iPad in front of him with my name written across it. Well, most of my name, anyway. I introduce myself and he immediately grabs my backpack officiously. "Allow me, Mr. O'Connell. And welcome to Montana. Do you have a checked bag today, sir?"

I tell him I do, and he insists on pulling it off the carousel for me. With help like this, I might be able to take it easy on Von's kettlebell workouts soon. Listen to me; one first-class flight and I'm already getting soft. Focus, Will. This is the big time. Act like you belong until you feel like you actually fit in.

Reggie—that's my driver, I learn during our chat in the back of his immaculately maintained Lincoln Town Car—takes me to the hotel where I'll be staying for the run of the film. The hotel staff seems to have been prepared for my arrival because I forgo the front desk and am instead privately ushered directly up to the top floor where the bellhop leaves me with a key to my room and the assurance that the film's production team has generously handled his tip.

When I say that this room is sweet, I mean it figuratively. But when I say it's suite, I also mean that literally because it's an actual multi-room suite. The front entrance welcomes me with a fruit basket and hand-signed card from the Madhouse Pictures Production Team. The room opens up into a sitting area, an office nook, a separate bedroom, and a sparkly bathroom. This place might be larger than my apartment in LA. It's definitely cleaner.

After I've unpacked and showered, the front desk calls to inform me that Reggie awaits me in the lobby to take me to set. My head reels from this new level of care and attention people are paying me. I booked the lead role in one feature film and all of a sudden, I'm being treated like royalty. They should treat teachers this way, I think to myself, as Reggie graciously holds the door to his Town Car open for me.

Arriving at the converted warehouse that the production team looks to be using for some interior scenes and as a base of operations, I am immediately greeted by the ebullient, if foul-mouthed, director.

"Liam, baby. You beautiful fuck. Welcome to Montana. Get over here!" Dennis wraps me in a firm hug, then grips me by the shoulders as he bores his eyes into me. "You look great. I'm excited. You excited? Of course you are. Come on, let me introduce you to your co-star."

Dennis ushers me toward a sea of people who part instantly at our approach, leaving a direct line to a face I'd recognize anywhere. Abigail Summers, Hollywood starlet and ultimate hyphenate—a star who wears all the hats in this industry from producing to writing to acting—stands firmly rooted to her spot, wavy blond hair somehow managing to move in this windless space. Her blue eyes sparkle and her smile instantly relaxes me. "This must be the soon-to-be-famous Liam O'Connell. Abigail Summers. Pleasure to meet you," she purrs in a voice that is somehow equal parts honey and vinegar. There is no denying her beauty—every magazine in America can't be wrong about that—but her background as a writer and producer speaks to the fact that there is much more to Ms. Summers than just a pretty face. And it is, I must admit, a pretty face.

Briefly, an image of my blackbird flashes through my mind as I extend an arm to shake Abigail's hand. I cannot wait to tell Raven all about this.

My now second-nature Irish accent falls effortlessly from my mouth as I smile back at one of the biggest stars in the entertainment industry. "It's an absolute pleasure, Ms. Summers. I'm a huge admirer of your work and very grateful for this opportunity."

"Flattery will get you everywhere, good-looking. And please, call me Abby." She directs her attention to Dennis, still beaming next to us. "If he acts as good as he looks, we might just be on the brink of something real special here."

"Just you wait, Abby," Dennis says with a huge smile, then addresses the whole room to get everyone situated for our table read. "Alright people, grab a water, grab a chair, and let's take a trip with Jett and Ruby, shall we?"

A few hours later, hours that have felt like minutes in my mind, the room falls silent as Avina, the assistant director, reads the final stage direction.

"We see a close shot of Ruby's hands, bloodied and bruised from the war they just endured, wrap tightly around Jett's sculpted midsection. He revs the bike once. We pull out to see him look Ruby in the eyes over his shoulder."

I look at Abigail as I deliver the final line of the film. "Hold on tight, baby. This is gonna be one hell of a ride."

Light laughter and a few sniffles can be heard in the room as the assistant director continues: "Jett and Ruby share a look before Jett faces the road and guns the engine. Lights fade on Jett and Ruby riding toward the horizon. Toward their future. End."

The crew, many of whom have been standing around the outside of the table this whole time, burst into applause. As do several of the supporting cast members. I take in the energy of the room, sharing a look first with Abigail, then the rest of the cast, and finally, Dennis who is all smiles.

"That's what I'm fucking talking about, people. We've got something here. We really fucking do. Everyone get some rest because we start filming this gem first thing in the morning."

Muffled conversations pick up as several people in the room offer me congratulations or words of encouragement.

As the chatter dies down and I've collected my things, one of the production assistants gives me the pages, call time, and rundown for tomorrow's shoot. A car will pick me up for hair and makeup at seven AM. Wardrobe at eight. And we are cameras hot at eight-thirty.

Abigail's entourage breaks up as I'm making my way toward the exit, and she reaches out to touch my shoulder. "Not sure how many of these you've done before, but that reaction? That doesn't happen often."

"That is nice to know. This is actually my first feature," I whisper conspiratorially, though I'm fairly confident she already knows that. Abigail Summers is the kind of woman who does her homework.

"Well, nice work, Freshman. I'm looking forward to going on this journey with you." Her tone manages both sincerity and flattery, professionalism, and a hint of flirtation.

Reggie swings me by a little deli so I can grab a turkey sandwich and a couple bananas. Then I'm back in my room to review tomorrow's pages and get some sleep. The falling asleep part takes no effort at all after this whirlwind day, but before my eyes close, I manage a message to the black-haired beauty fast ascending my phone's favorites list.

> **Me:** Hey Blackbird. This is me writing to say goodnight. This is also me, writing to say, that thing I told you before I left? I meant it. I've had all day to think about it, and my thoughts on this have not wavered. Just wanted you to know that. No pressure, just confirming facts. And also, I wish you were here. Today was awesome. My co-star is super friendly and seems very supportive. (I have a co-star WTF?!) And the table read went great. Can't believe I started this day at an ostrich farm with you! Longest. Sunday. Ever. Anyway, this text message has officially become an email at this point. I'm off to bed. Will check in tomorrow between scenes. Sweet dreams Rave.

I set the phone on my nightstand and my eyes are closed before I even get a chance to read her reply.

CHAPTER TWENTY-FOUR

THE NICE THING ABOUT MISSING RAVEN'S REPLY TEXT LAST NIGHT is that it means I get to start my day reading her words to me. That's a habit I could get used to real quick.

Raven: Good night, Liam. Or Good morning, depending on when you read this. So glad to hear things are off to a great start. I just know you're going to be dynamite.

She closes that message with a wow face and stick of dynamite emoji. I had no idea those silly graphics could make me feel this good. Then I read a second text she sent a few minutes later.

Raven: My inbox is always open for you, Liam.

And damn, I have never been so turned on by email in my life. The wink and black heart emojis that follow that text do more than put a huge smile on my face. I adjust my crotch before grabbing my bag to head downstairs for my first day of filming.

The first day becomes the fifth day in the blink of an eye. Film sets are their own ecosystems, like their own mini countries. The director rules over his kingdom. The cast and crew abide by the kingdom's laws and serve the will of the ruler. Hours mean nothing and time doesn't play by the same rules on set. It's a twenty-four-hour machine that grinds forward chewing up pages of script and consuming gallons of coffee along the way.

Things are admittedly rosier from my vantage point. Every location comes with its own trailer. I have assistants that will get me whatever I need and three people assigned specifically to make sure my sandy brown hair lays just so, my lightly tanned skin does not shine under the lights, and each and every outfit hangs off my muscular frame in the most flattering way.

As exciting as a film set can be, it can also drag. Lighting, sound, hair, makeup, set design: the cogs in this machine are myriad. Each aspect of production has to be set, then double-checked for every shot. Filmmaking is a beautiful, though painfully inefficient artistic medium. This leads to a lot of 'hurry up and wait' for the actors. That has meant plenty of time for me to familiarize myself with my lines and develop a solid rapport with my fellow actors, particularly Abigail, who sits across from me in my trailer now, sipping hand-torn Jasmine green tea. "The natural tearing of the leaves enhances the flavor," she informs me.

"I'm a coffee man, myself."

"Oh, I thought tea was big in Ireland."

I take a quick breath, reminding myself that Liam is the one on set, not Will. Never a moment to let my guard down. "Common misconception. Just one of the many things the British ruined for us," I make up quickly, not sure if any of that is true.

Abigail raises an eyebrow. "You're good, you know." I swear, my heart stops beating. She knows. She's just caught me, and she knows and it's all over.

"Pardon?"

"On film. In the scenes. You're really good."

"Oh. Thanks. That's a huge relief." In more ways than one.

"All the best actors are coming out of Europe these days, aren't they?"

And immediately that seed of doubt returns and grows inside me. Would Abigail think I was any good if she knew I was just some kid from Southern Ohio? Would anyone?

"The training is rigorous," I deflect.

"Don't take this the wrong way, but your accent helps."

"How so?" I ask, her question adding water to that growing bud.

"It's warm, inviting. Then you snap into Jett and well, frankly, it's exhilarating. Arresting even."

"Can't do much arresting without handcuffs," I joke to try to diffuse the energy.

"I'm sure I could track down a pair," purrs one of the most beautiful women in the world. This isn't an exaggeration. She's on lists for this kind of thing all the time.

And although it seems pretty clear that I could make a move on Abby right now, or at the very least, ask her out for drinks later, the thought doesn't even fully cross my mind. Because Abigail Summers may be the most beautiful woman in the world, but she's not the most beautiful woman in *my* world. There's only one woman who has my vote.

"I don't imagine my girlfriend would be too keen on that," I tell Abigail, bringing Raven into the conversation since I can't bring her into the room.

"Ah, the Irish sailor has an anchor, does he?" Abigail asks, sounding amused. She does not seem disappointed. Honestly, this woman never seems ruffled. Probably part of her success.

"I do. Raven."

"Oooo, I love that name. Did you know a group of Ravens is called an unkindness?"

"Well, this one must fly solo because she is probably the kindest woman I've ever met. And the prettiest. And most thoughtful. And one of the most talented. Present company also on that last list, obviously."

"Flattered, Liam. Thanks. Must say," she continues on a light laugh, "you sound pretty taken with this girl. One might even say in love."

"I would. I would be one of those people who says that."

"Wow. Ok. Good for you. Does she know that?"

"Told her right before I flew up here."

"How'd she take it?"

"Didn't say it back, but that's ok. That's not why I told her."

Abby appraises me thoughtfully before speaking. "You're alright, Liam. I can see why you're a good actor."

"What do you mean?"

"You're not afraid to commit. Not afraid to be vulnerable. It's dangerous. But no one falls for the folks who play it safe."

Abigail finishes off the rest of her tea and brushes a soft kiss on my temple as she exits my trailer. Leaving me thinking to myself, if only she knew how committed I am.

CHAPTER TWENTY-FIVE

THE NEXT MORNING THE CREW AND I ARE ON LOCATION AT JETT'S hideout cabin filming some of my solo work. The afternoon and tomorrow morning have some of the only scenes on the schedule that I'm not in, so I've made plans to have a FaceTime dinner date with Raven.

After spending my morning chopping wood and living off the land for the camera, I'm excited to get back to the hotel and spend the evening with my woman.

My woman. God that feels good to say, if even just in my head.

When eight o'clock rolls around, I have everything set up for our virtual date. I have thoroughly missed spending time with Rave, so I am pulling out all the stops to make this evening special. As I run wet fingers through my hair to tame my wavy locks, I double-check the collar on my slim-fitting denim button-down. Feeling and looking good, I head to the dining table in my hotel room's sitting area and call Rave from my tripod-mounted phone.

She answers on the first ring and that's the last full breath I take. Even trapped on the other end of a four-inch rectangle, my blackbird soars. Her creamy white skin contrasts so beautifully against her straight, dark hair. Her warm brown eyes drink me in and her sinfully red lips have me wanting to look up the first flight back to LA.

"You look…incandescent." The words rumble out of me like an ocean wave pounding against jagged rocks.

"You clean up pretty nicely yourself there, Mr. O'Connell."

The spell breaks momentarily when my phone cuts the feed to show an incoming text. "Shit, sorry. Need to put this thing on Do Not Disturb," I say, tapping away on the screen to make it so no one can interrupt my evening with Raven.

She does the same on her end and then grabs the chopsticks sitting atop her Pad Kee Mao. "Oh good, the food arrived."

"It did indeed. You got me Sapp Coffee House Thai. Very impressive."

"The plan was to get myself Thai as well, but that is harder to come by in Billings, Montana, so I had to settle for veggie Lo Mein."

She smiles, then twirls some flat, wide noodles onto her chopsticks. She holds it in front of the phone, offering me a 'noodle cheers,' then we each take a bite.

The soft moan her first bite elicits sends blood shooting straight to my dick, and instantly my hunger intensifies. Though stir-fried noodles are no longer what I'm after.

"Good?" I ask to fill the silence and stop my mind from wandering.

"Euphoric," she purrs.

"Jesus fucking Christ, I've never been jealous of food before."

We both laugh and slip easily into conversation—Raven telling me about work and her upcoming TikTok video plans—while I fill her in on all things *Nowhere to Hide.*

Just one short month ago, I could never have imagined any of this: filming on location, a career on the rise (hell—a career AT ALL!), and most importantly, a woman with whom to share those successes. I cannot describe the full-body joy I feel when Raven looks me in the eyes and tells me, "I'm really proud of you, Liam. Sounds like you're making the most of this incredible opportunity."

"I'd like to make the most out of this evening together too, if you're game." I hedge with a bit of rasp in my throat.

"What did you have in mind?" Raven asks in a tone that tells me she's up for anything.

"Well, I'm not going to lie. I miss you. A lot."

"I miss you too, Liam," she agrees, and I continue, speaking almost over top of her.

"Physically. I mean I miss you a lot of ways, but right now, I'm talking about the way you smell, the way you taste, the way you touch, the way you make me feel."

"Oh yeah? And how do I make you feel?"

"Good. Fucking great. The way you touch me makes me feel like I live in a world without gravity. Just fucking floating, Rave."

"That sounds real nice," she hums and there is no mistaking the heat building behind her eyes.

"I want you, Blackbird."

"You can have me, Liam. Any fucking time you want."

"How about now? You wanna play with me?"

"Yes, but I'm not gonna lie. I've never done this before."

"Neither have I," I tell her as we consider entering these uncharted waters together.

Raven suggests we put headphones on and retire to the bedroom, so I pull my phone off the tripod and take her with me to our separate beds. Both of us are now lying down, phones held over our faces.

"Mmmmm," she moans softly as her head hits the pillow and the intimacy of the headphones amplifies the lust in her voice.

"It's so great to see you," I say and the emphasis I put on the *so* drips with need.

"You too," she rasps, a hint of shyness I so rarely see in her and I definitely don't want to do anything that will make her uncomfortable, so I offer her an out.

"We don't have to do this if you don't want, you know? Just talking with you is fucking incredible."

"No, I want to, this is just new to me."

"Me too, Blackbird. But I've been thinking about your smoky vanilla scent and your vampire lips for a week. So, if this is the only way I can have you right now, I'm damn willing to try."

"Vampire lips? You think I'm going to kill you, Liam?"

"No, but I think you could suck me dry and make me feel immortal."

"Jesus, Liam. How are you turning me on this much from a thousand miles away?"

"Can I ask you something?"

"Anything."

"Right now, I'm pretty curious if you're wearing a bra under that Green Day t-shirt, and if so, what it looks like."

"Oh," she pouts playfully. "Did you want to find out?"

"Yes, please."

Momentarily, the screen gets blurry as Raven uses both hands to remove her top, so I take this opportunity to do the same, leaving me in nothing but a pair of navy-blue boxer briefs.

When her face returns to the view screen, we are both topless and she giggles when she sees me.

"I couldn't wait," I said. "Hope that's ok."

"It's more than ok. You look delicious. I could eat sushi off that chest."

"I wish you could fucking eat me right now."

"I would bury my face in your neck right now, run my fingernails across those firm pecs."

"Shit, Rave. That sounds fucking incredible. Your heavy breasts pressed against my stomach. Jesus."

"Speaking of...." And on a sly smirk, she slowly pans the camera down to give me an eyeful of her two handfuls. She runs a hand over each of them, cupping underneath and bringing them together for me.

"Do you know how perfect your body is?" I ask earnestly, taking in the curves that run down the side of her breasts and into her narrowing waist.

"You make me feel like it is."

"Good. Because it is. I'm so hard for you right now."

"Seeing is believing, Liam." Raven arches one eyebrow.

"Oh, I'm only too happy to comply," I say as I sit up slightly in the bed and tap the button to switch the camera from facing me to facing out. I can still see Raven's porcelain doll body, but now she has a view of the v lines of my abs as they point straight to the bulge in my center. I take my free hand and slowly play with the elastic of my underwear. I give my package one firm squeeze, then draw my thumb under the waistline and slowly, fucking achingly slowly, slide the underwear down my length. First revealing a tuft of hair, then the base of my length. I pull the fabric away, revealing more of the topside of my dick for her.

"Holy fuck, Liam. That's hot as hell. Look at that throbbing vein. You look so fucking big."

"You do this to me, Blackbird. All you."

"I am enjoying this view of all of you, let me tell you." As she whispers this to me, I slide the boxer briefs the rest of the way down my length as the head springs free and slaps against my stomach before I take a firm grasp of myself and stroke the length once, sharing all of myself for her.

"Jesus, Liam, I am so wet for you. Your dick is fucking perfect," she moans reverently.

At her lust-filled words, precome kisses the end of my cock and I continue to stroke languidly.

"Show me how wet you are, Blackbird. I want to know what I do to you," and my voice has taken on a darker, controlling tone. She has unlocked something inside of me, a lustful part of my personality only she has the key for. And fuck if that doesn't excite me even further.

Her camera travels down to reveal a landing strip of hair outlined enticingly beneath a ridiculously sexy pair of polka dot cotton panties. The colors from the dots bounce off the white of the fabric, the white of her skin, like streetlights reflecting off rainy pavement.

She brings her other hand over the top of that sacred V, then rubs two fingers down between her legs. She lets the camera follow from her side, tilted at an angle that still allows her a view of my stroking while giving me a forbidden look at the dampness soaking her.

"My god, Raven, you're a fucking siren."

"What do you want me to do, Liam?" She encourages me to take the lead and I'm only too happy to oblige. The carnal thoughts pouring through me, unbidden, but very fucking welcome.

"Slide your finger along the side of that seam and pull those panties aside. Let me see you glisten."

My obedient girl does not hesitate, slipping the fabric into the groove of her left inner thigh, giving me a full view of her. The strip of black hair that travels down her snow-white skin inviting me to the pink wetness below sends my whole body into a frenzy. I wish I could touch her and smell her right now, but there's something so erotic about these limitations.

"Like that?" She purrs.

"Yeah, Rave. Just. Like. That." I emphasize each word in turn before continuing. "Now slide those fingers up and down that slit once. Coat that clit in your wetness and paint your body in slow circles."

"Liam, that feels fucking amazing. Don't stop."

"Let me see you. Don't stop circling that clit, but I want to see your tits and look at your face."

I leave my camera trained on my cock, giving her a few moments to watch me pleasure myself. The hunger in her eyes at the sight of me has my balls tightening already. I tap the camera flip button so she can see my face. Lust radiates off me.

I stare through over a thousand miles and drill my hazel eyes into her browns. "I love watching you feel good, Blackbird. Your pleasure turns me on so fucking much."

"Fuck, Liam, I'm close already."

"I want to come with you, Rave. Will you come with me?"

"Yes, baby. I want to. So badly."

"Good girl. I can't wait to see you erupt. Now show me that perfect pussy again so I can see what it's like for a finger to disappear between your thighs."

Raven obliges as she spreads her legs farther, then curses and shimmies as she pulls her panties all the way off. "Fuck those things, they were getting in my way."

Then she stills her camera arm again as she cups her mound and slides two fingers in and out of her core.

I flip my view back as the pace of my strokes picks up speed. Our hands now match each other's pace, doing our best to imagine we're sharing the same bed right now.

"Oh Liam, I'm there. So close."

"That's it," I coax in a low, needful growl. "Don't fucking stop, Rave. Fuck yourself for me. That's it, baby. Don't fucking stop."

"Fuck, Liam. Fuck, I'm cooooming," she moans as her thighs begin to quiver.

"Show me your face. Right now, Raven. I want to see your pretty little face." She instantly complies, treating me to a face in a state of pure bliss as she watches me stroke furiously.

"I want to see you come, Liam. Please. Please. Please," she pants on breathy moans, still in the throes of her orgasm. Her eyes roll slightly back into her head as her neck cranes skyward. When her eyes find the screen again, my cock rewards her with shots of pure ecstasy coating my stomach and drenching my hand as I let out a low "fuuuuuuuuck" from the darkest corner of my fucking spirit.

"Oh my god," she praises as her breathing starts to slow. "That was…"

And neither one of us has the energy or brain power to finish that sentence. I keep stroking my shaft, the lubrication from my come momentarily intensifying the effect before becoming sticky.

I turn the camera back on my face because I need to see her now. She needs to know, if not with words, then with a look, how intense, how passionate, how real, that felt to me.

After several breaths, I know that this is not enough, so I tell her, "You are fucking incredible. Thank you for sharing that with me."

"The pleasure was all mine, Liam. Wow. That was better than most of the sex I've ever had."

"Yeah, I don't want to talk about any of the other sex you've had, but I'm damn glad to hear that."

She giggles softly as she says, "Noted."

"And for the record, same," I tell her with stone-cold honesty. We hold a silent moment together on the line before I am forced to break it. "I really need to go clean up right now," I say, and we both laugh.

"Totally," she replies. "Me too. Will you get a chance to call me tomorrow?"

"I will make the time. Promise."

"Sounds great. I look forward to it."

"Me too," I say and we both smile.

"Goodnight, Liam."

"Goodnight, Blackbird. I fucking love flying with you."

With that, I end our call, zombie walk to the bathroom to clean myself, then float back into bed for some of the best sleep I've had in a long, long time.

HOLLYWOOD

CHAPTER TWENTY-SIX

ANOTHER SET WEEK FLIES BY. I MADE GOOD ON MY PROMISE TO CALL Raven that next day, but since then, it's been nothing but texts between scenes. Before leaving my trailer, I fire off a message to Raven.

Me: How is the prep for your show going?

It's several hours before I'm able to look at my phone again, but her reply makes the wait well worth it.

Raven: I'm working on new looks every night. Helps that my boyfriend is out of town becoming famous. I can really stay focused!

She sends a few pictures of some revealing and expertly crafted concert tees.

Me: Hope these come in my size. They are hot!

Raven: Thanks for checking in. You're sweet. Means a lot to hear from you. Now get back to work!

Her affirmation fills me with newfound energy. These twelve-to-fourteen-hour filming days grind on and definitely take their toll. And my excitement about my future with Raven is definitely one of the things keeping me going. There's someone else who's partially responsible for my being able to keep up with the rigors of production. The realization that I owe Von a huge thanks for kicking my butt and keeping me in the kind of shape I need to be in, not just to look fit on camera, but to keep up with the physical demands of shooting.

I fire off a quick text to him to say as much because I think it's important to celebrate those folks in your circle. Worst thing you can do for a friend is to say something nice about them at their funeral that you never got around to telling them while they were alive. I always try to let my people know they're valued.

Von responds immediately with a flexing bicep emoji which in Von's world means 'Thank you, I feel appreciated.' It is also a gentle reminder that the dude has killer arms. He is jacked.

Just then, Skyler, one of the production assistants wraps on my trailer door to inform me that lighting is now set, and we are ready to roll on the next scene. When I return to my trailer a few hours later, a series of texts from Devontay sits on my notification screen.

> **Von:** Dude, you're officially buzz-worthy now. Gossip columns out here talking about your movie before it's even done filming.

Scrolling down I see a link to the article in question. I click on it and begin to read:

> Leaked footage from the set of Dennis Lawson's new romantic thriller has America abuzz about Hollywood's next IT guy, Liam O'Connell. Stills from the set show this brawny Irishman glistening in the Montana woods and an interview with his Oscar-winning co-star, Abigail Summers, quotes her as saying he's one of the kindest and most present actors she's ever had on a set. This authorized clip shared exclusively with *The Hollywood Minute* shows a hint of some of the range that his director has been going on about…

I decide not to click on the video since I do not want to get self-conscious about my work and watching myself at this stage of the game can only serve to get into my head. My eyes keep returning to the word 'Irishman' in the article as the realization of how big this lie is becoming starts to dawn on me. Not only is this fabrication standing firmly between me and Raven, but it's now also becoming a very important part of the brand I'm inadvertently building. I just hope when I remove those Liam bricks the whole building doesn't collapse along with it.

INTERLUDE #5

We All Love To Play Pretend

HEY, STITCHES! LET'S BE REAL. ALL WE WANT IS TO BE ROYALTY. ALL we ask is that the world sees us as superheroes. We spend our childhoods in a beautiful land of naïve make-believe, then spend our adult lives chasing down those fantasies, trying to reclaim them. Well, I've got a secret for you, my friends: Clothing can help.

That's right.

We don't think about it this way, but what is your outfit other than a suit of armor you wear every day to protect against the slugs the world fires at you. We're all just out here rocking tops, bottoms, and accessories to turn ourselves into princesses, superheroes, frogs, snakes, whatever we need to try to realize our own self-expression in this unimaginative world. Well, stitches, you go on and feel free to dress yourself not just for the job you want, not just for the person you want, but for the whole gosh darn WORLD you want!

Ok, now that I've got you all thinking about all your clothes as potential costumes, let's turn our attention to today's project: Making An Actual Costume.

Let's say you meet a guy, and that guy is pretty wonderful. Then let's say that guy has an adorable niece who happens to have a costume party coming up for her birthday. What better way to show you care (and maybe impress the guy and his squeezable niece) than by throwing your hat in the ring to make her a one-of-a-kind dragon ensemble to make her the belle of the ball.

Well, in this totally hypothetical land of make-believe, here is what you'll need to make one seriously powerful, pretty, purple dragon: glitter, felt, Velcro, a hoodie and some sweatpants, and your own magical gift—your unshakeable belief in the power of your creative energy.

Step-by-step instructions at the link in the comments. Come back and share your creations because magic is stronger in groups. Bye!

CHAPTER TWENTY-SEVEN

As we head into the final day of filming, the morale on set feels sky high and our intrepid leader Dennis assures us we will wrap tonight, on schedule—a virtual unicorn in the land of filmmaking. Over-budget and past deadline are basically industry standard for most pictures, I've been told, so the knowledge that I'll make it back tomorrow with one evening to spare before Lexi Bean's, or should I say Lexi Sprout's, big seventh birthday bash puts my mind at ease.

Getting back to see Raven is also pretty front of mind these days. It feels like forever since our FaceTime call, mainly because it has been. Almost two full weeks since we've done more than text and although I haven't had time for more, it has not been nearly enough. This time apart has also done nothing to diminish my feelings for her, that's for sure. I've been filming in the wilderness with a Hollywood legend. Any one of her fifty million social media followers would give an arm to spend this time with Abigail and I would trade places with any of them if it meant getting me back to Raven sooner. Abigail has been wonderful though, I must admit. Ever since our chat in my trailer, we have not had one moment where our on-screen chemistry or on-the-page romance has clouded our judgment or fogged our off-screen friendship.

Raven Locke consumes my waking thoughts and my nightly dreams. This entire filmmaking experience has been the culmination of so much hard work. It's so incredible to be an integral part of this storytelling machine. A dream come true. So many of my dreams come true. But something happened. A Blackbird has flown into my life and nested squarely in my heart. And the simple fact is that I cannot imagine any of these dreams without Raven in the picture.

But that picture is still out of focus because I haven't been able to let Raven all the way in. Haven't let her in to the real me. Even though my feelings for her are genuine; in spite of the fact that I have only ever shared truths about my passions and my desires; I have been honest behind this mask, but everything remains cloudy because I have been behind this mask. She deserves to know the truth no matter what it might mean to my career. Because I respect her, I value her, and I cannot imagine this life without her in it.

I told her I love her because I meant it. I do. But I cannot expect her to share those feelings until I take off this mask and let her see the real me.

Tomorrow afternoon. When I get back to LA. No more putting it off.

I send her a text to make sure she's still planning to pick me up at the airport.

Just as her response of "Can't wait. I will be the one in baggage claim with the gold balloons and giant smile" pops up on my screen, an incoming call from my agent rips my mind into the present.

"Liam, darling. How's my little four-leaf clover?" She opens before I can even say hello.

"Good, thanks, Molly. Filming has been absolutely amazing. I'll be back in LA tomorrow."

"I know, that's why I'm calling. Listen, Liam. You didn't hear it from me, but there has been some Emmy buzz for your work on *Boise Patrol*, and when you get back we need to hit the ground running."

"What?" I exclaim, momentarily slipping my accent at the sheer astonishment of what she's telling me. I recover, slightly, as I continue. "An Emmy nomination? Are you serious? For my TV debut?"

"Nothing is set in stone, but there are a few things we can do to capitalize on this momentum."

"Yeah, sure. What can I do?"

"I made some calls and I got you a slot on *Strong Words with Kerri Strong* next Monday."

"Are you serious? That's the number one late-night show in the country. That's incredible."

"I know, Liam. What can I say? I am very good at my job. Seems you are too, hotshot." Molly manages to sound totally matter of fact about all of this. "My assistant will send you some talking points and directions to the studio in an email later today. Call with any questions. Take the weekend to relax because we go hard on this and figuring out what's next for one of Hollywood's rising stars on Monday. And don't worry, I will be at the taping to walk you through everything. Oh, and Liam? The show films at five in the afternoon. Don't let the eleven PM airtime fool you."

"Right. That makes sense. Thanks, Molly. I'm speechless."

"Well, don't stay speechless for long, Irish. That accent of yours should make for some fine talk-show television."

She disconnects before I get a chance to respond, her comment about my accent momentarily resurfacing all those Imposter Syndrome feelings. Then a bigger, bolder thought takes hold. The largest television audience in America. What better place to set the record straight? That's certainly no way to reveal myself to Raven, but I can have that conversation with her the moment I return to LA ahead of Lexi's birthday party, like I'd planned. Then Monday, I have a chance to tell the rest of America, and Will can take over where Liam left off—no more hiding. After proving myself on set these past few weeks, I feel confident enough that I can pull this off without destroying my career.

Several hours later, Abigail and I hold for one last closeup as we sit astride Jett's motorcycle. After a weighted beat, the entire cast and crew are greeted with one of the sweetest strings of sentences in all of filmmaking. Dennis pops his head up from the monitor like an excitable groundhog and belts out, "Cut. Print. And that, ladies and gentlemen, is a wrap on principal photography. Nice work, everyone."

Abby immediately breaks character and touches my shoulder with a warm smile. "Really great work, Liam. It's been a pleasure working with someone of your caliber. They just make 'em differently on your side of the pond, I guess. Can't wait to do it again." She swoops in and plants a soft kiss on my cheek as she slides off the bike toward her trailer.

And the elation of wrapping my first film deflates within seconds as Abigail's comment drops on me like an anvil. Not for the first time, Devontay's words echo in my mind, and I am reminded that I did not think this through. But—I remind myself—I am thinking now, and I have my plan.

That evening the Madhouse Pictures team treated the cast and crew to a private party in the hotel's ballroom. Drinks flowed as freely as the compliments while everyone congratulated each other on a successful shoot. If the energy in the room is any indication, *Nowhere to Hide* might be something that people *everywhere* will attempt to *seek*. (I should definitely leave the puns to Devontay).

The next morning, I enjoy my last room service breakfast compliments of the production company as I let the cheesy eggs and turkey bacon sop up some of last night's indulgences. The slight nausea I'm feeling, though, definitely has more to do with the conversation I'm planning to have with Raven the second I land, rather than the countless whiskey sodas from the night before. Not that I'm not ready to have this talk, I am. It is long overdue and I know it, but I just want it to go smoothly. Or as smoothly as it possibly can, I suppose.

With my bags packed and the drawers of my hotel room compulsively checked and re-checked more times than I care to admit, I join Reggie downstairs. He first picked me up at the airport and is now here to see me off.

In the car on the way to the airport, I shoot off a series of texts.

To Von: to tell him about the Emmy buzz and to set a workout schedule for the week.

To Lexi via Ryan: to tell her I cannot wait to see her at the Dragons and Dinosaurs bash.

To Raven: to tell her how much I've been looking forward to this reunion.

Though that text does not feel like enough, so I immediately call the top number on my favorites list, and Raven's warm voice answers on the first ring.

"I was just writing you back," she says by way of greeting.

I tap into my Irish accent for the last time with Raven and feel relieved about that. Next time I speak to her, it'll be as Cincinnati Will. "Text did not seem sufficient. I cannot wait to see you. Wanted you to hear it from me."

"I do love hearing your voice, so this is a welcome call."

"How is the prep for the OooLaLa show going? Happy with the progress you've made?"

"You are so sweet to ask, Liam. Honestly, you wrapped principal photography on your first feature film and you're already asking how my silly little art show is coming along."

I balk at her insecurity. "Not silly at all, Blackbird. It's a big fecking deal. I cannot wait to watch you shine."

"You make me feel pretty sparkly already."

"You're glitter to me. See you in a few hours."

We hang up as Reggie pulls me up to the curbside at the airport.

Wheeling my bag through the carpeted terminal, I feel a bounce returning to my step. Sending those messages and talking to Raven reminds me of all the love I have waiting for me in Los Angeles. And when I see the heart emoji from my Blackbird pop up on my phone, my nerves about this talk with Raven get tamped down by hope. A firm belief that Raven will know that what we've built is real and we can grow from here.

Together. Nothing hidden. Just raw, honest truth.

An hour later, as the plane takes off, my mind races through the final touches of this plan. This evening will mark a new chapter in my story with Raven. She will know the real me and we can build on that foundation together. Beginning at my niece's birthday party which we can attend without any lies—the only masks we'll wear, the ones for our costumes. My family no longer roped into my convoluted backstory in the name of my career.

By Monday, with my core group firmly behind me and my belief in myself firmly rooted to my family and my love for Raven, I will be ready to face the world and come clean about everything.

And celebrate Raven's successes alongside mine. Because one more thing has become crystal clear; her dreams live right alongside mine now. Her triumphs even more important than my own. With these thoughts swirling, I nod off in my cushy, first-class seat, ready to face my future.

CHAPTER TWENTY-EIGHT

If 'hope is the thing with feathers,' then once that plane lands and my phone boots up, I instantly became an eagle.

A *bald* eagle. Not a feather in sight.

Between the missed calls, text messages, and emails, I have more notifications than I can count. Everyone in my orbit and plenty of people I do not know have all been trying to get in touch with me. I weed through all the noise clogging up my phone and find my text chain with Devontay, knowing he always gives it to me straight. "Sugar isn't good for your body, so I won't ever coat anything in it. That's a promise," he's fond of saying.

I tap the bold outline of his name in my messaging app and see two new lines of text. The first reads:

Sorry, bud. Looks like UR fucked.

Below it, there is a link to an article on *The Hollywood Minute* titled 'Irish Up-and-Comer Nothing More Than a Midwest Downer'.

I go to the article, though the headline certainly doesn't leave much to the imagination. Certainly seems to tell a complete story, I think sardonically, as my stomach plummets when I see my face next to the headline:

> Fresh new thing Liam O'Connell may indeed have the Gift o' the Gab, but he did not get it from his childhood in the Land of Eire. According to sources close to Mr. O'Connell, whose first name is Will, he actually came to Los Angeles by way of Cincinnati. That puts his place of birth only about a hundred miles away from Dublin... OHIO. But a few thousand more from the capital of Ireland.
>
> Long-time acting teacher and former child television star Lenny Schneider shared footage timestamped from just earlier this year showing Mr. O'Connell on stage discussing a scene with no accent anywhere to be heard. "The kid has talent, I'll give him that," Mr. Schneider said. "But an Irish passport, he does not."
>
> Additional research from our team unearthed his birth certificate from Mercy Hospital in southern Ohio.
>
> William O'Connell has recently been hailed for his dramatic turn in an episode of *Boise Patrol* and finished shooting his first feature film, *Nowhere to Hide,* in the Montana wilderness. This magazine was unable to reach Mr. O'Connell for this article, but we have no doubt he is now desperately searching for *some place* to hide.

A momentary flash of annoyance that *THM* managed a perfectly solid *Nowhere To Hide* pun, gives way to rising rage.

What the fuck, Lenny? I think to myself as I feel the blood draining from my face. And then all I feel is dizzy. And nauseous. And fucking terrified. As fast as my career ascent was, the whole thing came tumbling down even faster. In mere seconds, everything is exposed. And I have no idea what it means. I simply cannot wrap my mind around any of this at the moment.

My body marches through the airport on autopilot as I make my way toward the exit, too numb to think, too shocked to do anything but put one foot in front of the other.

Then, as I make my way past the security checkpoint and walk into baggage claim, I finally become aware of my surroundings. Or, more specifically, what's not in my surroundings.

No balloons. No giant smile. No Raven.

CHAPTER TWENTY-NINE

I CANNOT TELL YOU EXACTLY HOW I GOT MYSELF TO THE CURB OUTSIDE Terminal 7, but the sun is beating down on my face and I am supporting my weight with the handle of my suitcase. I am here, I have all my things, and I am still in one piece. Von pulls up in his black Jeep, breaking me out of my fugue state. I truly cannot remember anything that happened from the moment I walked into a Raven-less baggage claim until now. I am not even entirely sure how much time has passed.

Devontay hops out of the Jeep, grabs my bags, and slings them into the back of his ride. He grabs my shoulders, appraising me, then locks me in a monster bear hug.

"Get in, idiot." That last word uttered with a tremendous amount of love.

Once he navigates us past the hellacious ring of traffic exiting LAX, he looks over to see my still stricken face. "You okay, man?"

"I honestly do not know what I am, Von. I'm just shocked." Then, after a beat, "Fucking Lenny," I say with more surprise than malice.

"Yeah, bro. Definitely not cool."

"Did not see that one coming."

"Don't underestimate the depraved hunger for attention in this city, Will. A pernicious disease out here, to be sure."

Then it hits me, and I feel terrible. "Yeah, I might have had something to do with it, actually. Now that I think about it."

"How?"

"I kinda skipped a class or two and then totally forgot to let him know I was filming in Montana and just bailed on last month's scene study. He emailed me the invoice and I forgot about it."

"Dude."

"In my defense, there's been a lot on my mind."

"Even more now, you—at the risk of repeating myself—idiot."

"Fuck, Von. I had a plan in place."

"Sounds like you might need to move up that timeline."

My mind starts racing through all the people I will have to answer to. All the drama still yet to unfold. I start rattling off names. "Molly, Dennis, Abigail, shit, the whole cast and crew of that movie I probably just ruined. You, Ryan, Lexi..."

"Hey, take it easy," Von interjects authoritatively. "We'll figure all this out. Let's just get to your place first."

I sigh, then utter one more name into the silence filling the Jeep. "Raven."

Von looks over to me but says nothing. What is there to say?

"I was going to tell her today, first thing. I fucking swear. Had it all planned out," I peter out as I glance down at my phone for the first time since leaving the airport. The screen opens on my messaging app. A string of unanswered texts to Raven stares back at me.

> **Me:** Raven, please let me explain.
>
> **Me:** I totally understand why you're not here. I just wish I could talk to you.
>
> **Me:** I never meant to lie to you. I never meant to hurt you. I swear. I was going to tell you the minute I got back.

Me: Please. Talk to me. Just, please, Raven.

Me: Please.

A short while later, Von has deposited me and my bags into my apartment. He helps me set up a game plan.

"You can't fix all of this at once, Will. One thing at a time, one person at a time. Let's make a list and start checking things off."

Von grabs a pad and pen off a desk and continues talking, seemingly aware that I still can't work my way through any of this. "Let's start with your brother. They'll be worried about you. Then probably call your agent, she's definitely going to be pissed, but she'll probably have some insights into—"

I cut Von off, mid-sentence, blown away by how quickly he is jumping in to help me clean up this mess. The very friend who was the most vocal in his opposition to this plan from the outset, stepping up when I need him most. "Thanks, Von. For all of this. You don't...and I mean...well, anyway, thanks, man. Truly."

"You already know," he says, looking me right in the eyes. "Now, let's get to work."

The ceaseless onslaught of emails and phone calls from unknown 323 and 818 area codes are constant reminders that I need a new, comprehensive game plan that doesn't suck this time. That means seeing how far my current cheering section extends. Staring at my phone, I swallow some of the last remnants of my pride and call my agent.

When her eager, young secretary answers with a "Molly Margolis' office, this is Derek. Who's calling?" The brogue comes back instantly as I respond, "Liam O'Connell."

"Oh," he says in response. Those two letters stretch out into a multi-syllabic grunt. "It's you. Thought you were from Ohio."

Devontay eyes me from his armchair across from me. "What the fuck, man?" He whisper-yells.

"I don't know. It was just a habit." Then into the receiver I snap back to my normal voice. "Yep. Sorry. Is Molly available?"

"I'm afraid Ms. Margolis is terribly busy with—my notes here say I don't even need to bother with an excuse. She doesn't want to talk to you."

"Um, ok. Do you happen to know if the taping is still scheduled for Monday?"

"Yep. Have it right here in our calendar. Four o'clock. Liam O'Connell's Funeral. Have a great weekend."

To punctuate his dig, the line instantly goes as dead as I feel. Not a great start.

After a brief moment to collect my thoughts, I hit the next name on my call list, ready to take as much punishment as needed to fix what I've created.

My brother answers his cell after a few rings.

"Hey, Will." The formality of his tone portends a rocky call.

"Hey Ryan. How's it going?"

"You sound like shit."

"I feel like shit."

"Well, if you called seeking comfort, this is the wrong number. I'm not exactly your biggest fan right now."

"I can understand that bro. I'm only calling to say I hope my presence is still welcome at Lexi's birthday party tomorrow. I will probably be attending solo, but also did not want to crash a good time."

"Not gonna lie, William. I'm pretty pissed right now. It's one thing for you to attempt this insane scheme, but another entirely to get a six-year-old to lie on your behalf."

Lie? Then our post-lunch conversation with Raven outside the Ralph Lauren store flashes through my mind and my stomach plummets through the floor as I realize just how bad that was.

"That was not cool," I tell my brother. "None of this has been cool. I am sorry about all of it. I hope you know how much I love my niece. Love all of you. Being there tomorrow would mean the world to me." That's all I can say at this point, so I leave it at that.

My brother lets out a huge breath. "My hands are tied, aren't they, Will? Lexi adores you and she'd be mortified if you missed her party."

"I would be too."

"Shut up."

"Ok."

"We'll see you tomorrow," he eventually relents. "But leave all that drama at the door. This day's about Lexi."

"Of course. Thank you, bro. I will be there, ready to serve the magical birthday dragon."

Ending a call with Ryan, I exhale for what feels like the first time in hours. It's not much, but it's progress.

Damage control underway, I glance at my phone one last time, willing a message from Raven to appear. But all the wishing in the world isn't going to change the fact that I fucked up the best thing that ever happened to me.

I thank Von for, basically, everything, then kick him out because the only thing left for me to do at this point is sleep. With thoughts of that fair-skinned vixen spiraling endlessly through my brain, I reach over to my night-stand to send one last text, figuring I can't do any more damage at this point.

> **Me:** Back in LA, but this city of eight million feels crazy lonely when the only person I want to see doesn't want to speak to me. I'm sorry. I have so much more than that to say. I know I don't deserve it, but I hope you'll give me that chance. Good night, Blackbird.

INTERLUDE #6

Know When To Fold Them... And When To Tear Them Apart At The Seams

Here's the simple truth, my stitches. Because all I can ever do is keep it real with you all. Sometimes, an outfit does not work. Sometimes, that bolt of fabric that looked like it would make a perfect skirt doesn't. Sometimes, what you envision in your mind does not translate to reality. The colors in your head, the patterns you laid together perfectly in your sketchbook? Well, sometimes, you put in the hours, you do the hard work of creating, and you know what? It doesn't turn out the way you thought it would.

So, what do you do then? I will tell you. You dig into your kit and pull out one of your most trusty tools... The seam ripper.

That's right. Sometimes, there's nothing you can do to save what you built, so you rip that bad boy apart at the seams and start again. Is it painful to start over? Of course it is, my beautiful stitches. You put time, energy, and passion into that piece.

But that fabric is too precious to throw away and you're not leaving the house looking a hot mess. So you grab that ripper, and you dismantle what's not working.

And. You. Start. Again.

HOLLYWOOD

CHAPTER THIRTY

If you have never tried to slip into an Apatosaurus costume in the back of an '85 Volvo, may I suggest that you don't. It is as difficult as it sounds and does nothing to alleviate an already sour mood.

I am quite literally pulling together the final touches of a dinosaur costume that was going to be half of the cutest couple in costume party history. Raven and I had been planning to attend together as a pair of vegetarian literary dinos: myself as A-Poe-tosaurus and Raven as Emily Brontësaurus.

But Raven still is not answering my messages and it's becoming pretty clear that my relationship has more in common with dinosaurs than I'd like to admit. Namely, that they are both extinct.

Reminding myself there is nothing to be done about that situation at the moment, I take a beat to focus on the positive before affixing the signature Poe mustache to my otherwise Jurassic ensemble. Today, my adorable niece turns seven. I get to be a regular part of her life, and I made good on my promise to be here for this extremely special day. I pull out my phone hoping to see a message from my Blackbird. No notifications, so I turn my camera on myself to make sure my costume is in place. Gray jeans and a textured gray thermal make up the body, while a matching balaclava with looping ears helps transform my head and neck. I did spring for the long sweeping dino tail which does not quite drag behind me. Probably should have gotten out of the car to put that on.

I hold my camera arm out wide to take in the whole effect, selfie-style. Upon closer inspection, I might look a little more like a sick coyote than a prehistoric titan, but hey, it's the thought that counts.

Smile affixed firmly to my face, I head into Ryan and Hazel's place to celebrate one of my favorite people. And am suddenly aware that I am the *only* adult in costume. No parent has even feigned an effort at a dragon or a dino. Surely someone at least had a *Game of Thrones* t-shirt they could have put on. Serious thoughts of slipping into the bathroom so I can slip out of the head wrap and tail are cut short in my mind as a lyrical accented voice rings out, "Will, you made it. So good to see you." Hazel glides over and wraps me in a hug, glass of rosé held aside.

"Hey, sis. Good to see you. Been too long. What's up with the no costume thing?" I ask, eyeing down her form-fitting spaghetti strap tee and jeans.

"Lexi's seven now. If her parents got involved, we'd just ruin it for her. It's a miracle she's invited us at all."

"Maybe I should change then."

"Nonsense. You can do no wrong. She'll love it." Then she shifts the conversation instantly with a look. Her eyes ask, along with her mouth, "How are you doing?"

"I am hanging in there. My agent has joined a growing list of people who won't speak to me, so that's a bit disheartening."

"So basically, just an agent, then." Hazel puts in.

"All her assistant would tell me is that I'm still scheduled to appear on *Strong Words* on Monday to attempt my huge *mea culpa*."

Hazel's eyes light up and she cuts me off before I can continue. "The *Strong Words*? With *The* Kerri Strong?"

"That's the one."

"I love that show."

"Everyone does. Let's just hope they love me on it."

"You'll do great. I believe in you," she offers, placing a comforting hand on my arm.

"Well, the only person I care about apologizing to after you and Ryan won't return any of my calls or texts, so..." I trail off as I reach for my phone out of mindless habit, even though I already know there are no new notifications.

"Oh, Will. I'm so sorry to hear that. And more than that, I feel I owe you an apology," she says before downing the rest of her rosé and placing it on a nearby table.

"No, sis. Don't be silly. You have nothing to apologize for."

"Well, this was basically my idea."

"It was *our* idea," I insist. "And it's my life. Choices I made; consequences I have to face."

"Do you want a drink? Sound like you could use one."

"No, but thanks, Haze. Trying to keep a clear head right now."

"Well, if there's anything—"

Hazel's earnest platitude is cut short by a blur of purple energy slamming into my legs. "Uncle Will, you made it," Lexi exclaims.

I get down on one knee, tail awkwardly smacking a chair behind me as I descend. "Of course I did, Sprout. No place I'd rather be."

"Mommy and Daddy made it sound like you are in trouble, so I didn't know if you would be here."

I throw Hazel a quick side-eye before returning my gaze to Lexi. "I am not in trouble, Lexi. Just made some questionable choices I need to answer for. I'm a grown-up and that's what we have to do sometimes. But none of that is important right now. What's important is *you*. Because it's your birthday!"

"It is my birthday. You're right," she crows. "Umm, Uncle. Can I ask you something?"

"Anything, Lexi Sprout. What is it?"

"What's up with that mustache?"

I laugh, having forgotten about the dark accessory on my upper lip. "I, my Dragon Queen, come to you today, but a humble dino servant." I stand and bow, regal British accent firmly in place. "Allow me to introduce myself. I am Edgar Allan A-Poe-tasauraus."

"Who was from Baltimore, not Brighton," Hazel interjects.

"I don't get it, Uncle Will."

"He's a writer. You'll learn about him eventually. It's—" I cut myself off, fully taking in Lexi's costume for the first time. "Never mind. Not important," I say as I pull the mustache off and stand to my full height. "But your outfit is awesome, Lex. Is that the one Raven made you?"

Saying her name out loud leaves a coppery taste in my mouth. Must be what regret tastes like.

"It is," Lexi beams, twirling around. Her outfit is an expertly sculpted dress with lace, jewels, and frills that give the effect of scales and dragon wings. The costume is somehow both effortlessly adorned and magically ethereal. A perfect look on the birthday girl. A perfect reflection of the costume's creator.

Disappointment and loss run laps in my stomach as I try to tamp down those feelings in front of the little. I allow my feelings of awe at the ensemble to take center stage as I smile and say, "You look awesome."

"Thanks. I love it. We weren't sure if she was still doing it, so mom had a backup, but then this came today. Special delivery. From a bike courier. On a Saturday! I felt like a movie star."

I laugh at Lexi's animated delivery of her monologue as she bounces around, showing off the wings and flying effects that she can create with the costume. Then a critical piece of her explanation dawns on me.

"Today?" I ask, looking at Hazel for confirmation. "That costume came today?"

"Yes, like Lexi said. Bike messenger. Picked it up in East LA at eight AM. Dropped off here by ten." She pauses to let my mind catch up. "Today," she reiterates.

That sense of loss stops whirling around my insides, replaced instead by a small spark, a tiny morsel… of hope. Raven may not be speaking to me, but she didn't forget about Lexi. Even after the truth of my duplicitousness came to light. Maybe, just maybe, she hasn't given up on me either.

"Hey, Lex, stand still. I want to take a quick picture of you."

Lexi halts mid-spin and strikes a fierce Dragon Queen pose, instantly finding the camera. I snap a great shot, then open my messages app. I attach the photo and fire off a text to Raven.

Me: The Birthday Girl looks radiant.

I pause before hitting send to think about what else to say. My fingers fly over the keys, adding simply, "Thank you." I hit the little blue arrow, offering a silent prayer as I return the phone to my pocket.

Just then Ryan comes over and shakes my focus back to the present with a fierce side-hug. "Nice costume, bro. What are you supposed to be? A dying dire wolf?"

Damn it, I think, as I'm swept back up in the spirit of the party, *that's even better than a sick coyote.*

A few hours later the party rages on. Von showed up and spent thirty minutes pretending to be an evil giant that a team of flitting dragons attempted to subdue. I oversaw a rousing game of Pin the Spikes on the Stegosaurus, and Ryan got the full rundown from me and Von before Hazel came over to help us brainstorm critical talking points for Monday's interview. Sure, my brother and his wife may have nudged me off this cliff, but they're also the ones waiting at the bottom with the net. Can't ask for more than that.

As we are winding down our chat, Lexi almost literally flies over. Kids are fast. "When's cake and ice cream, Mommy?" Lexi asks.

"Five minutes, Sweet Pea."

"Ok, thanks." Then she turns to go, but immediately turns back around and asks the assembled adults, "Is five minutes a long time?"

My instinct is to answer with a simple 'no', but Hazel chimes in first. "That depends on your perspective, baby."

"What's that mean?"

"Well, if you are watching a movie or spending the day at the park, then five minutes is not a long time during the course of all that fun. But," she continues in impressive professorial mom mode right now, "five minutes is a super long time if you're trying to, say, hold your breath under water. So, time is relative."

"Sometimes it's fast; other times it can feel achingly slow," Ryan adds in.

"Well, I really want cake and ice cream," Lexi states, elongating the word 'really' for maximum emphasis.

"Sounds like it's going to feel like a long time, then. But it will be here before you know it," Hazel concludes and Lexi, seemingly satisfied, runs off to join her friends again.

The three of them continue talking, but my mind bores into the exchange Hazel and Lexi just shared. I can't stop myself from fixating on this notion of the fragility of time. Time itself might be infinite, but my time most certainly is not. And it has never been more clear in my mind that I want to give my time, however much of it I have, to Raven. I know I fucked up. I can only hope she'll give me an opportunity to make amends. An opportunity I know I need to earn, to beg for if I have to, because a future without Raven? That time would creep along at a snail's pace.

With these thoughts pouring through my mind, a buzz in my pocket brings my attention back to the moment. I pull my phone out to see a new notification, the only notification I have wanted to see for days. One from Raven Locke.

'Raven Locke likes a photo.'

My entire body warms as I click on the notification seeking the visual proof of that message. There, stamped digitally into the upper left-hand corner of Lexi's adorable costume picture, hangs a little red heart. But that elation is short-lived. That balloon of hope instantly bursts as I read the incoming message from Raven.

Raven: I'm so happy. For her.

CHAPTER THIRTY-ONE

I STARE AT MY PHONE. DEFLATED. DEFEATED. DESTROYED. AN ADDItional message does not follow afterwards. I stare at my phone willing it to spark to life with another text from Rave. But all that hoping manifests nothing. At least not now. My immediate circumstances take me out of this digital cave as it is now time for cake and ice cream.

Those five minutes went achingly slowly for me, by the way.

Lexi blows out the candles that have been expertly placed inside the mouths of several fondant dragons and angel food cake castle towers. Dessert is passed around and while I don't have much of an appetite for anything right now, I manage a few bites in the spirit of celebration.

Lexi proceeds to open more presents than any child could conceivably use in a lifetime, let alone a single year. Von and I pitched in to get her a royal evening with the family at Medieval Times figuring that one awesome present was better than two smaller presents. I also always try to get my friends experiential presents rather than physical objects. My friends like to claim that's just so I can tag along on their birthday present fun, but I really just think making memories is more fun than collecting stuff. Lexi beams when she opens our 'royal invitation'. Von and I share a look. We did good.

Once the guests have all left, the remaining four adults help clean up. At her parents' insistence, Lexi places two of her brand-new toys off to the side. Those presents will be donated in new condition to a local shelter. Some might think it's rude to turn around and give away a present that someone thoughtfully picked out specifically for her, but Lexi's birthday has netted her a mountain of new toys, while, as her parents often remind her, other kids are not nearly as fortunate. So, as a birthday and holiday tradition, two brand-new, never used toys make their way to a new home. Gotta say, my niece definitely lucked out in the parent department. Just as I have been deeply blessed with this awesome family, from blood and from bond.

Those thoughts of the family we make send my hand involuntarily reaching for my phone again, the screen tauntingly blank. With a muffled sigh, I return the device to my pocket as Von asks if I want him to add my name to the guest list at some influencer's brand party at a warehouse in San Pedro.

"I don't think there's a single thing you said in that sentence that appeals to me," I say, my thoughts of Raven bleeding into my other interactions.

"A simple 'no thanks' would have worked just fine, man."

"Sorry," I apologize sincerely, if half-heartedly.

"I get it, brother," Von responds as he squeezes my shoulder, then heads for the door.

My own exit follows a few minutes after Devontay's. I grab my tail and DIY-dino head which had been abandoned hours ago, offer a quick round of goodbyes to my brother and his family, then head back over to the other side of the 405. Nothing but a generous plate of leftovers and my ceaseless thoughts of Raven to keep me company.

INTERLUDE #7

Memories for Mañana

NOT GONNA LIE, MY FAITHFUL CUT CREW, THIS HAS TO BE ONE OF the hardest videos I've made to date. Why? For today's tutorial, I want to talk about making clothes from memory. And no, I'm not talking about learning these steps by heart and repeating it. I am talking about taking some of your treasured items, those keepsakes from your past—good and bad—and turning them into something new.

You may have heard of women repurposing their wedding dress into a skirt, a piece of lingerie, or even a tablecloth for their parents' living room. Because hey, why not? It's not like you're going to wear the thing again and finding a new way to love that gown, finding a fresh form for it to re-enter your life, sounds like a hell of a lot more fun than leaving it to hang for decades in a closet.

Whether it's turning a couple of your grandpa's old sweaters into a plaid mash-up cardigan to remember a lost family member, or a midi skirt made from that box of old baby shirts your mom kept in the basement forever, finding a new way to breathe life into those past items can help bring those positive feelings back to life.

Whenever you're thinking about building a new memory piece, I encourage you to start with something you already love. For me, I'm looking at this denim jacket that's given me years of style and comfort. Today, with some scissors, thread, and a few selections from my closet—like this baseball jersey—that remind me of a certain time, a certain person in my life, I am going to transform this into a vision board or a voodoo doll. Only time will tell which way it goes…

CHAPTER THIRTY-TWO

TURNS OUT HARRY NILSSON ALSO HAD IT RIGHT: ONE *IS* THE LONEliest number. Sunday came and went in a fog. My first trip back out on the water in almost a month was not the peaceful, connective moment I've come to expect from that weekly paddle boarding ritual. All calming breaths were thwarted by thoughts of Raven's knowing laugh, each steadying shift of my hips jolted by visions of the California sun reflecting off her soft white arms like diamonds. And like diamonds, the memories cut because I'm afraid there won't be any more. They blind because I'm becoming increasingly convinced, I won't see her again. After watching what she did to her baseball jersey on TikTok, I think I can safely assume my invite to her OooLaLa! opening tonight is no longer on the table.

A knock on the door pulls me out of my head and drops me like a ten-pound sack of potatoes smack dab into the middle of my reality. That reality being that "We are two minutes to places, Mr. O'Connell," the bubbly PA announces, peeking her head around the green room door. I try to shake those thoughts quite literally from my mind as I shimmy my shoulders and bounce my head back and forth on a quick inhale of breath. Standing from my chair, the cavalcade of moments that led me to this exact place washes over me like the first big wave of a winter swell—beautiful to look at, but fucking painful to be caught up in.

A few months ago, I was nobody. My identity, real or otherwise, did not matter to anyone in this town save for my core group of family and friends. One crazy idea born of frustration and plain old guilelessness led me down a road that ascended straight up the mountain. From nobody to working actor, working actor to film star, in quick succession. But even as I reflect on these insane professional milestones, meeting Raven in that wardrobe studio is the vision that crashes hardest against the rocks. Landing the lead role in my first full-length feature a gentle lapping at my feet compared to the riptide of emotions I feel when I think about every minute I've spent with Raven.

Right now, I find myself seconds away from having to answer for my brazen behavior. From having to ask for America's forgiveness and understanding in front of the largest nightly audience on television. When in my mind, in my heart, there is only one person whose forgiveness and understanding I care about.

I stand rigid behind a red velvet curtain. The applause of the live studio audience muffled slightly by the heavy fabric in front of my face. I check the partially and deliberately half-rolled sleeves of my crisp untucked Oxford more out of nervousness than vanity.

"We are stand-by for go," the same PA from the dressing room informs everyone. My heart rate climbs as I try to steady myself with some deep breathing. On an inhale, Dennis's first directing notes from the set of *Boise Patrol* flash back into my mind. "Focus on pursuing your character's objective. Figure out what he wants and go after it relentlessly. Do that and the rest will take care of itself." Alright Dennis, I will do my best. So sorry I lied to you.

As the applause crescendos, Kerri's liquid voice pours above the noise and fills the space. "Ladies and gentlemen, my guest tonight would have needed two forms of ID to get into the building a few short months ago, but now needs no introduction. You can catch him this fall in the upcoming feature *Nowhere to Hide* starring opposite Abigail Summers. Or you may have seen him last week in a stirring episode of *Boise Patrol.* In more recent news, you may have seen him plastered across every Hollywood tabloid. We'll get to all of that tonight, so please give a warm welcome to Liam O'Connell."

Kerri draws my name out just slightly, inviting the audience to cheer as the curtain draws apart and I step unknowingly into the abyss.

I keep a smile on my face and my shoulders pressed back as I walk just a few short steps across the stage that feels miles long. Kerri stands to greet me with a warm smile and firm handshake. Her buttery soft skin and inviting brown eyes would be calming, if her energy did not somehow simultaneously give off serious alpha predator vibes. Think Wendy Williams' approachability with Viola Davis' intensity.

"Please, have a seat. So good of you to come on the show."

"Thrilled to be here, Ms. Strong," I say, my Irish persona abandoned, trying now to get used to using my normal speaking voice in public again.

"Call me Kerri," she purrs. "Speaking of which, let's dive right in, shall we?"

She continues, Cheshire Cat grin painted across her face, before I can say anything. "What should I call you? Liam? Or would you prefer to go by Will now?"

"Liam is fine, thanks. My full name is William, so it's my attempt at a playful stage name. Like Topher Grace, you know?"

"Sure thing, Liam. Only, as far as I know, Topher didn't fabricate a back story to get himself cast on *That 70's Show.*"

"Straight into the deep end, then, I take it," I joke, adjusting my legs.

"It is the thing on everyone's mind right now. Your leaked audition tape from *Nowhere to Hide* has over two million views online. In that clip, we see you asking the director questions with a noticeable and if I may say, delicious, Irish accent. Then as if a switch is flipped, you dive into an extremely believable Midwest accent. So authentic, in fact, that it turns out it was just your natural speaking voice."

"Yes, that's right. I hate hearing this story, I just feel awful."

Kerri continues digging the knife in. "America started to warm up to the charismatic Irishman who could transform into a broody backwoods rebel in the blink of an eye. And then we found out it was all an act. Do you have anything to say for yourself, Liam?"

"Sure, ok. That's fair. Yes, yes I do." I take a deep breath to tamp down my nervous rambling. "I only have one thing to say: I am sorry. I have no interest in lying anymore or sugarcoating anything that's happened over the past month or so. I let my frustrations over a failing acting career lead me to a place where I made some seriously questionable choices. I lied. At first, I thought it would be totally harmless. But as the days wore on, and more and more people on and off camera started to get to know this fabricated persona, I realized how deep of a hole I'd dug. I'm just sorry, Kerri. That's all I came here wanting to say. To Dennis Lawson for taking a chance on me. To the production companies that trusted me to be a part of their projects. To everyone on the cast and crew."

One person in particular, I think to myself, though I don't say any more about that. I turn my hips in my chair then fix my gaze on the camera in front of me, as I finish my plea. "To everyone involved, from the bottom of my heart, I am, truly, so very sorry."

I take a breath and return my attention to Kerri who appraises me earnestly. The audience's silence is palpable as they seem unsure whether or not to boo or applaud my declaration.

Kerri breaks the ice. "That was an extremely heartfelt apology, Liam. I must say, in this day and age, it's pretty refreshing to hear someone take responsibility for their mistakes and simply ask for forgiveness. No deflection, no bluster, just an honest apology." A smattering of applause rings out as Kerri asks another question. "But I guess I'm still a little confused, Liam. Why? Can you tell me why you did this? You're clearly a very talented actor. Hell, your work on this Irish character might be even more impressive than your work on-camera, so why did you do it? Why not trust that your talent would take you there."

"Well, let me start by saying, thanks for those kind words. Being called talented by an entertainer of your caliber is one of the highlights of my career, even if that career does end tonight."

"The jury's still out, Liam. Talk to us about what you were thinking."

"To be honest, I felt like I'd run out of options, and it was either try something new or give up. And I *really* didn't want to give up." I place a huge amount of sincere emphasis on the word 'really'. "Acting is what I've always wanted to do. And I honestly believe I've worked really hard to be good at it. I moved to LA the second I was able to because this life called to me. The life of a storyteller. It's brave and timeless. And I know tons of people feel that way and this industry chews up hopes and dreams for breakfast every single morning, but these are *my* hopes and *my* dreams. I guess I just wasn't ready to give up on them."

"Well, Liam, I think many of us can appreciate a lot of what you just said. This business is ruthless, no doubt about that. If you knew half the things that went on behind the scenes before they'd give a black woman a shot at hosting a late-night talk show, it would make you cringe. But what was the endgame here? How did you see this playing out?"

"Not this way, I can tell you that." I feel a huge weight lift as I laugh along with the audience. "I figured if I could land a few roles, get a bit of a resume together, then I could quietly come clean or even simply slip out of the accent, but keep the name I'd built for myself. Whatever you want to call me, whatever name I go by, the work is still mine. And I hope that speaks for itself. I just needed to get my foot in the door. I needed that first big break. And instead of waiting around for it, I tried to make it. It's like my friend, and awesome personal trainer, Devontay Williams, says, 'If you're not prepared for success, then it won't matter when opportunity comes knocking.'"

"I like that. Sound advice. Well, I gotta confess something, Liam O'Connell. I came into tonight's interview ready to embarrass you on national television. But you seem alright to me. I don't know, what do you all think, America?" Kerri turns her attention to the studio audience who immediately break out into applause.

I can feel my shoulders finally start to relax as I feel the tide shifting in my direction. I just might live to see another day on-screen.

"You heard 'em, Liam. I think America might be willing to give you another chance. Great news for the folks at Madhouse Pictures too, since I know they've already invested quite a bit into *Nowhere to Hide*."

"For the first time in the past month, Kerri, I am speechless."

"I think we can all understand doing just about anything for your dreams. And hey, it's not like you took a pipe to anyone's knees or anything like that."

Another round of laughter fills the soundstage as visions of Raven crash back into my mind. This interview has gone as well as could have been expected, better than I'd hoped for honestly. But that emptiness returns to my chest instantly at the thought of the person I wronged most of all. Before I have a chance to think better of it, I interrupt the light mood in the room with a question.

"Actually, Kerri. That's not entirely true. Do we have time for just one more apology?"

"We need to head to our commercial break, but we can hold for a minute. What did you want to say?"

"Well, you're right that I thought what I was doing was something of a victimless crime. When I went into this, I assumed the only person I could hurt was myself. And that was a chance I was willing to take. But then I met someone."

"Uh-oh," Kerri interjects, leaning closer in her chair. "Plot twist."

"I met someone. And unfortunately, we met under these false pretenses."

"She thought you were actually Irish?"

"Right."

"And once you got going, you couldn't stop the train."

"That's pretty much it, yeah. And the thing of it was that as my feelings for her grew, and man did they grow. Fast. My fear of what would happen when I came clean got more intense. Because I wanted that relationship to work more and more. I had planned to tell her, but it didn't happen. She found out about my accent and my fake backstory the same way everyone else did, and she hasn't spoken to me since."

"Ouch, that's rough, Liam. Did you want to say something to this person?"

"I just want her to know how sorry I am. That I never meant to hurt her. In fact, I'd do anything I could to protect her from pain because I feel so strongly for her, that I can't feel joy unless I know she's okay. I would trade all of this for one more date with her. If I could do this all over again, I would probably attempt this fake Irish scheme again, but not because of what it's meant for my career. Because it's how I met her. I'd give all that up in a heartbeat, but I never want to give *her* up."

My speech is delayed momentarily by a soft chorus of 'oohs' from the audience, then I continue. "And if I destroyed any chance of her forgiving me, I would understand that. If she never wants to speak to me again, I will learn to accept that. But I need her to know how sorry I am. Nothing in this world is worth the price of taking the smile off that beautiful face." A pause. "Thanks for letting me say all that, Kerri."

"You're very welcome, honey. Guess the ball is in this mystery woman's court now."

Another laugh and applause from the audience before Kerri turns up the show-woman charisma. "Well folks, this has certainly been an enlivening discussion. You can see him later this year in Madhouse Pictures' *Nowhere to Hide* and who knows, I've even heard there is some Emmy buzz for his *Boise Patrol* performance. Think it's safe to say this won't be the last we see of my guest, Liam O'Connell. We'll be back with our musical guest after a word from our sponsors."

Red lights throughout the space all blink off and Kerri's shoulders relax as she places a hand on my forearm. "Nice work, young man. And I know I just met you, but between me and you, I hope she gives you another chance. You really do seem alright to me."

I offer Kerri a huge smile and sincere thanks, then walk down the buzzing hallway to my dressing room. My relief momentarily halted when I see a flash of dark hair rounding a corner backstage. Could it be?

I run down the hallway, past my dressing room door, and turn that same corner. The woman walking away is unmistakable. I would recognize her anywhere. From behind, from the side, from the front, Raven is imprinted on my memory and my heart. Everywhere.

"Raven," I call, hope and desperation lacing that one word. Liam's accent is retired now. Replaced by my own, the only version of myself I ever want to offer her again.

Hope dares to swirl as Raven turns and marches toward me. She does not speak, but instead stands toe-to-toe with me, looking impossibly larger than her five-foot-four-inch frame.

"You came to the taping." I state the obvious. "To see me?" I ask, still daring, still dreaming.

"So this is what you actually sound like." She opens the wound as she opens her mouth.

"This is what I sound like," I relent. "I hope you know how sorry I am. I meant everything I said on that show."

"Well, I *hope*," she begins, throwing the words I used right back at me, "that public apology does wonders for your career because it's done absolutely fucking nothing for me. You lied to me. About everything. And now you used me on national television to get people's sympathy."

Shocked, I start, "No, that's not—" But I know there's nothing I can say right now to make this right. My words don't even slow Raven down at all.

She continues as though I never even spoke. "I hope your fans forgive you, Liam, but I sure as hell cannot. There's no coming back from that. Goodbye, Liam."

On those painful but not altogether undeserved words, my body goes arctic-cold as Raven turns on her heel and walks straight out of my life.

CHAPTER THIRTY-THREE

Stunned, heartbroken, I remain frozen in place for who knows how long until enough feeling returns to my body that I am able to drag myself back to my dressing room. Raven is gone. And she is not coming back. I will never know if I was enough for her because I never gave her the chance to decide for herself. Cocky and cowardly in equal measure and always about the wrong things, I have no one to blame but myself.

Before I can make sense of any of it, the situation or my emotions, my dressing room door crashes open and my agent Molly tornadoes into the space, talking a mile a minute, face buried in her phone. I brace for my next verbal smackdown.

"Liam, darling, you're a genius and a charmer and I don't know how you did it, but that couldn't possibly have gone any better. When this thing airs in a few hours, your career is gonna take off right along with it. You're hot, you're likable and you're damn good-looking. Paul Newman good-looking." On this, she glances up briefly from her phone to pinch my cheek.

She continues talking, her snubbing of me the other day forgotten, it would seem. Agents, am I right?

As Molly continues praising my performance and laying out a continued game plan to get our "Emmy buzz"—as she calls it—back on track, my attention shifts to the door as Von walks in. He's quiet enough not to interrupt Molly's monologue, but the eye contact we make tells me all I need to know. He thinks I did good.

I sigh, and ask him, "Yeah?"

Molly pauses and turns her attention his way. Von confirms, "Yeah, man. You were you. You were Will, or whatever name you want to go by. It was genuine, man. And the stuff about Raven? I'd certainly hear you out."

"She did not feel the same way. Saw her in the hallway after taping. She was here." I let out a sigh, trying to control my emotions. "Now she is not."

"That sucks," Von states, master of brevity.

Molly, who has been typing furiously on her phone during this exchange, stops tapping and appraises my tall friend, perfectly centered in the door frame. "And who is this chiseled hunk, Liam?"

"Oh, uh, this is my best—and extremely talented—friend, Devontay Williams. D, this is my agent, Molly Margolis."

"And what exactly are you good at, Mr. Williams?" Molly asks, shark-agent morphing with cougar-mom.

"I specialize in stunts, train in mixed martial arts, and am interested in doing more work in Mo-Cap, Ms. Margolis."

"Call me Molly," she hums, offering him a business card as she slithers past him. "And do call me. I want you to meet Vince, our CGI department head. I think he's going to love you." She shouts back to me as she ambles down the hall, "Great work, Liam. Talk tomorrow after this airs. *Ciao*."

Devontay and I stare at each other dumbfounded for a moment before I break the silence. "Well, that connection is definitely a cherry on this shit sundae."

"Um, yeah. I hope you don't think I'm trying to—"

I cut him off mid-sentence. "Stop it, man. You kidding me? I wish I could have told her about you a year ago. But she didn't know my name until last month."

"She still doesn't, Cyrano."

Von's dig—while admittedly pretty funny—gives me an idea. It may be too late for me to get Raven back, but it's not too late to do right by her. I'm going to need some help—if I can get it. I send a quick text message before grabbing my things and heading out.

"Thanks for agreeing to meet me," I say to Abigail as she blows into Brü Coffee on Vermont. Abby's energy is reluctant but responsive as she offers me two air-cheek kisses then sits down in front of the green tea I ordered for her. "They don't hand-tear the leaves. I asked. But they said it's good."

"I miss the accent."

"Me too, Abigail. Felt like my armor. This side of me feels real fucking exposed."

"Why'd you do it, Liam?" I appreciate her forthrightness and openness.

"I was a big fat nobody, Abigail. Felt like I had nothing to lose. It honestly never occurred to me how out of control it would get. And the people. I didn't think about the people I'd meet. I've really enjoyed getting to know you, and I hope you accept my apology for lying to you. I understand if you can't, but thanks for giving me a chance."

Abigail bores her eyes into mine like only a fearless storyteller can. She pulls my innermost thoughts from me on just that look. "I get it, Liam. I'm sure we'll be able to move past this. We have a movie to promote together after all. Give it time."

I could be throwing away my last chance at salvaging a good working relationship with Abby, but I don't hesitate. Raven is more important. "That makes this next part a bit trickier then. I asked you here not only to ask your forgiveness, but also to ask you for a favor."

In the face of Abigail's coolly hostile gaze, I tell her my plan.

CHAPTER THIRTY-FOUR

THAT NIGHT, AROUND THE SAME TIME MY *STRONG WORDS* INTERVIEW is airing to the world, I walk to the entrance of a non-descript, boxy building. While my career finds its way slowly back on track, my focus is now on making sure that Raven sees every success she so richly deserves. I look up at the crackly pink neon sign that flickers 'OooLaLa!', the only indication I'm in the right place. I take a deep breath, then enter the big, open warehouse in Downtown's Arts District. The inside contrasts sharply with the understated exterior. Here, lights and sounds vie for my attention from every angle. The lofted space awash in color and music. From graffiti murals to appropriated Banksy prints, this place oozes contemporary counterculture. Artists from a variety of backgrounds employing tons of different mediums all proudly display their creations while a DJ spins his own brand of electronic funk artistry.

I move deliberately and inconspicuously in my slim-cut gunmetal gray button-down, dark jeans, and custom Chucks. As I turn the corner of one aisle of stalls, I stop short in my tracks as my eyes catch sight of Raven's booth.

A mannequin proudly displays the Stallone jacket she designed. The torn denim acts as the centerpiece of her setup. A memory of us discussing that very piece over ice cream flashes in my mind, but I tamp it down. I am not here for us. I ruined that. I am here for her. She does not deserve to be ruined.

Two other statues adorned with Blackbird originals bookend that signature design from an iconic film. Squaring off the space are a few clothing racks of items for sale and in the center of it all, a hypnotic vision of bone china skin and enticing features. Her violinistic curves rival any other piece of art in this building. Her body its own piece of music I could listen to and play all night.

But those future symphonies we could write together are not meant to be. I tore that sheet music apart with lie after lie. I know that. That's not why I am here.

Just then, a surprise visitor glides into the *Rags to Raven* pop-up space. Well, a surprise for Rave; I knew this person was coming because I am the one who invited her.

Abigail Summers commands a space as though cameras follow her every move. Perhaps, because they do. Whether Abby was always a star or morphed into the role, I do not know, but she certainly has the part down now. She floats down the aisle of vendor booths, eyes intent on the Stallone jacket I told Abby to look for to find Raven's booth. Raven's work looks incredible—so does she—and Abigail came through for me.

For the briefest of moments, I entertain the notion of walking over there and inserting myself into this situation. But this is not my moment. It's Raven's.

That's all I need to know. This isn't about me. And when you're not a part of the story, sometimes you gotta write yourself out of the scene.

So I do. *William O'Connell exits stage right.*

The long drive back to my place helps me avoid the constant barrage of texts on my phone. The influx of 513 area code calls a reminder not only of where

I came from, but perhaps where I am headed. Friends and so-called friends have all come out of the woodwork to say they saw me on television. Good, bad, or indifferent—I am somebody now.

And the cruel truth is a simple one. I would give up my fame for another chance with Raven. I drown that thought out with sound. I crank the stock speakers of my Volvo as much as Rita can handle and let Twenty-One Pilots try to heal the *Tear in my Heart*.

When I get home the tenor of the bulk of the messages makes it clear that my performance on Kerri Strong's show was well-received. No. Performance is not the right word because for the first time in over a month, I wasn't acting. Those words were genuine, that plea for forgiveness sincere. My career, according to my agent and a slew of other people, is now back on track.

My life, however, has been completely derailed. I set those thoughts aside for now, to find out if my plan was a success. All I asked of Abigail was to show up. That was all I *could* ask of her. Whether or not Raven and her artistry spoke to Abby would have to happen on its own merit, but I'm sure with her talent, it did. I am grateful to Abby for giving her a chance and hopeful that Raven made the most of it. I unlock my phone screen to find out.

INTERLUDE #8

Abigail Summers Live

CIAO BEAUTIES. IT'S ME, YOUR GIRL, ABBY. WHERE AM I TONIGHT, you ask? Well, you already know it's fab because I'm there. And because this event is sponsored by OooLaLa! Need I say more? No, I do not. But I needed to jump on this live to introduce you to the belle of this ball. This event is nothing but fire with so many people bringing so much talent, but this girl right here is the mothafuckin' Sun. She scorchin'.

Introduce yourself, Queen.

"My name is Raven Locke. I'm a wardrobe coordinator for several tv shows, I run the Rags to Raven TikTok channel and I'm an aspiring fashion designer."

You can drop that 'aspiring' word, honey, because these pieces are gorge. How do you make all this?

"I design exclusively from found materials. Everything you see here has been repurposed from other pieces. Brought together to make a new story for anyone that believes in second chances. The only new material I add to the mix is thread."

And love. *kiss* *kiss*

This piece I am buying. This one I am gifting. And all of these are here for now. Ladies—like, comment, follow, subscribe, and support. And if you're in LA, get down here before you can't afford any of her work!

Ciao, beauties.

CHAPTER THIRTY-FIVE

I DID NOT SLEEP WELL LAST NIGHT. BUT I DID SLEEP. THE PAIN OF NOT knowing, the chorus of what-ifs had me tossing and turning, but the look of joy, the hint of pride in Raven's voice on Abigail's video was a welcome balm. Eventually, the feeling that Raven's night ended better than her day had begun helped my head rest heavier on my pillow.

This morning, the ocean called me back and I started my day seeking balance within the ceaselessly moving. Calm in the restless waters. Feet planted, knees bent, mind clear—I remain standing. Some days that's good enough. Some days that's fucking monumental. Today, I celebrate the small victories. I did right by the person I wronged most. For her, not for me. I took steps to remedy the numerous relationships I damaged.

Maybe today I will start believing in my own gifts. Maybe today I will begin to see Will or Liam or whatever name I go by as enough. Not an imposter hiding behind a mask; a storyteller willing to lay his pains bare so that some may find empathy and comfort.

The abrupt caw of a seagull pulls my focus and unearths my balance as I fall off my board and go crashing into the cold surf.

Well, there's always tomorrow.

As I return to my spot on the beach, the green messages notification illuminates my screen, Raven's name written improbably across my phone. The message I find inside even more impossible.

Raven: Let's talk. Tonight. 8 o'clock. My place.

Moisture in my eyes may mingle with the saltwater dripping down my face as that feathered fuck creeps back into my heart: hope. When I settle my shaking hands enough to type a reply, I opt to keep it as simple as possible.

Me: I will be there.

I stare at the screen in disbelief for a few moments then impulsively fire off one more message.

Me: Thank you.

Raven's reply is instantaneous, tempering my expectations.

Raven: Don't thank me yet.

At five minutes to eight, I parallel park Rita on a side street in Echo Park and walk around the block to Raven's place. The brief walk in the crisp evening air gives me a chance to steel my nerves. Armed with a bouquet of wildflowers, a bottle of pinot grigio, and a heart full-to-bursting, all for the woman on the other end of that door, I take one more breath, exhale, and knock.

As the door swings open, my heart jumps firmly into my throat. She stands in the doorframe, arm outstretched holding the door open, her body a silhouette of dizzying curves that have my entire body taut, heated. Anxiety swirls with desire as my whole being is overcome by the mere sight of her. In a simple ribbed black tank top and gray sweats, her light skin and dark hair a stunning reflection of all of Raven's complexities and dualities. I, quite simply, have never felt this way about anyone in my entire life. And the singular thought now jackhammering through my brain is this: please give me just one more chance.

My overwhelming urge to reach out to her, to touch her, to kiss her—that urge is squelched instantly by the daggers shooting from her sharp eyes, her expertly sculpted eyelashes only adding emphasis to her hurt and disdain. I remind myself in the face of the weighty tension between us that she invited me here. I hope that means the future of our relationship, like her front door, is still open, if heavily guarded.

Nothing for it now but to speak. "Hi, Raven," I utter plainly.

Her eyes become two slits as she appraises me. "Come inside." Her arms break from the door, and she makes room for me to enter. I walk into her empty living room.

"Willow not home again?"

"Meditative Yoga retreat in Ojai. What do you have there?" She nods her head toward my hands.

"Oh, um. Flowers...for all the things. And the wine I am hoping we can share eventually, but if that's not how this goes, then I thought you'd appreciate having it either way."

"Give." She takes both from my hands and retreats to the kitchen. I am left standing in limbo as I hear her opening the wine and pouring. I throw my voice to the kitchen. "I was going to bring Merlot because apparently that name derives from the French word merle which means blackbird, but I know you prefer white, so I figured I'd opt for taste over poetic symbolism."

Moments later she returns with one glass of wine which she carries with her to the sofa. She sits cross-legged on the center cushion and motions to an armchair with her glass.

"Sit."

I do as I am told.

"The flowers are very nice," she continues in a flat tone, sipping from her stemmed goblet. "So is the wine."

"Good. I'm glad. It's just a small—"

Raven cuts me off, the ice in her veins chilling the whole room. "This was a bad idea."

"What? Why? No. Please. I just want to talk to you."

"You don't sound like you. Do you know what a mind fuck that is? Like, your voice is different from the person I met. Different from the person I dated. Different from the person I started—"

This time she cuts herself off and I fill the space with a plea. "It's still me. I swear. My name is William O'Connell. I'm twenty-six years old. I think Maya Rudolph is a national treasure and that you should only root for your hometown sports team. I love to read and have fun outdoors. Everything I told you about me was as honest as I could be. Always."

"Except your country of origin and your natural fucking speaking voice, Liam. Will. Whatever the fuck your name is!" Raven erupts, setting her wine glass down on the coffee table in frustration.

"I wanted to tell you, Rave. I swear I did. I tried. Multiple times. But something always seemed to get in the way."

"How could you let it go on this long? How could you let me find out this way?" The anger remains, but her tone begins to carry more hurt and something that sounds like a desire to understand. I want to believe she's trying to give me a chance here. "If you really cared about me, you would have told me. You would have, Liam."

I'm about to tell her that I was going to as soon as I landed, but that will just start a new argument. So, being a storyteller, I do what I do best instead.

"There's this bodega near my place. I stop by regularly for snack food and kombucha. The guy that runs the shop is this super-nice dude from Yemen who always tells me about his family back home and asks how my acting career is going. His name is Moogeeb. But at some point early on, he got my name confused and started calling me Bill. For years now, I've been going into this shop and his face lights up and he says 'Bill, *Hamdallah,* so good to see you.' And I guess at some point I missed the window where it would have been okay for me to correct him, and now we know each other too well that I don't want to embarrass him, so whenever I go into the store, I just answer to Bill."

Raven's fangs return as she drones in a monotone, "Moogeeb sounds very nice, but you still sound like an asshole. What's the point of this story, William?" She takes a steadying sip of wine, then sets the glass back down on the coffee table in front of her.

"The point is that Moogeeb still knows who I am. He still knows about some of my hopes and dreams. I know about his wife and three kids that he sends money home to every month and that he's working on getting their visa paperwork in order soon. He may not know my real name, but we still have a real bond. We know each other in the ways that matter."

I pause, hoping some part of this story has thawed her icy exterior. I continue, bringing my focus back to the woman who has been the center of all my spare thoughts for over a month now. "And that's how I have felt with you this whole time. And I did try to tell you before I left, and yes, I know that's not enough. And I honestly had boarded that plane back to LA ready to tell you the night I arrived, and I know that doesn't totally matter now. But I hope you know how much I've thought about you. About us. I wanted us to be able to move forward and I knew that wasn't possible until I gave you my full truth. That I'm just some nobody from suburban Cincinnati and not some international movie star from Dublin."

Raven takes a small breath and I try not to fixate on the rise in her chest. Just one of the million parts of her I've missed these past few weeks. When she speaks, she offers me a small kindness. "You're not a nobody. You've never been a nobody to me."

"That's not what the voice inside kept telling me. I wish I understood and accepted that earlier. I wish I didn't think I was such a fraud."

"Well, you might be a fraud, to be fair. Turns out you might now be a movie star, too."

"I would give all that up in a heartbeat if it would make things right with you. I would trade every second of it if it meant you'd give me a second chance," I say as earnestly as my fool mouth can muster.

She looks deep into my eyes. "Did you know Abigail Summers came to my booth last night?"

"I did see that online, yes. I am so happy for you. It looked incredible."

"I sold every single piece of clothing I had there."

"I am so happy for you," I say easily. It's easy to say things that you mean.

"Someone even offered me ten thousand dollars for my Stallone jacket."

"What? That's unreal. Did you take it?"

"No. I love that thing. And now I know it's worth ten G."

"No doubt."

"Woke up to over twenty thousand new followers and an inbox full of design requests." Her tone remains guarded, almost like she's interrogating me more than she is celebrating.

I am only too happy to celebrate for her. "That's the best news, Raven. You deserve it. All of it. Good for you."

A beat of silence, then Raven asks what we both know she's wondering. "Did you have anything to do with that?"

My turn for a moment of quiet reflection. Then I tell her the truth because the only way forward with Raven is honesty. "I did. I thought about lying to you right now because I really don't want any credit for this, but I do not ever want to lie to you again. Ever."

I think I see a hint of a smile crack her armor. I continue, "I met with Abby after the Kerri Strong interview to apologize and ask a favor. All I asked was that she stop by and look at your stuff. That's all. The rest was all her. And all you."

I can almost physically see her shoulders lift with pride at that fact. A confident Raven is by far the sexiest Raven. "Thanks," she finally says.

"As I said, you deserve it."

Some new thought seems to cross her mind and she tacks in a slightly different direction. "Can I ask you something?"

"Anything."

"How did you do it?"

"What?"

"Like, just practically speaking, how were you able to shift in and out of that character so easily?"

"Oh, um. I don't know. I think that's something I've been doing my whole life. My brother Ryan used to make fun of me all the time as a kid because I would always slip into these different characters or voices. But I've always had a natural knack for impersonations. If we ever met someone with an interesting accent or something, I would start parroting their sounds back in my own voice. Most of the time I didn't know I was doing it until someone pointed it out to me."

"The Chameleon Effect," Raven states with a hint of wonder.

"What?"

"That. What you're describing. Psychologists call it The Chameleon Effect. They hypothesized that people who subtly mimicked another person's behaviors would be more likable to that person. That people would do it subconsciously in order to be liked."

Instantly, it feels like a missing puzzle piece slots into place. Like I know myself more than I ever have before. Those feelings of inferiority, that sense of being an imposter, has an explanation. That comfort I found, that courage I felt behind that mask, has a reason.

"Wow. I never knew there was a term for that. I'm kinda blown away, honestly."

"You are definitely a chameleon, Liam O'Connell."

"Gotta say, I like that a lot more than Ryan calling me Gorilliam." I deflect with humor because I cannot process all of this in a single moment.

Raven laughs softly and I didn't even know how much I needed to hear that sound until she made it. "God, I've missed that."

"Hmm?"

"Your laugh. Your smile. You."

"Yes, well, I was doing plenty of that until the other day."

"Yeah, I know. I don't know how many times I can tell you I'm sorry."

"Don't worry. I'll let you know when it's been enough." Her tone offers a sliver of light, an olive branch. Or at least an olive twig.

"Does that mean you're thinking of keeping me around long enough to do all that apologizing?"

"I'm entertaining the idea." She reaches for her wine and takes another small sip, her eyes having taken on a contemplative haze. "Besides, it's not like you're the only one who kept secrets in our relationship."

A million possibilities invade my imagination, each more difficult to imagine than the last. "Have you been keeping something from me?"

"Yeah, something I also hadn't gotten around to talking about yet, I guess you could say. Deflecting."

"Ok. Well, no pressure, but I am definitely here whenever you want to tell me whatever is on your mind."

Rave takes another powerful inhale, then seems to weigh her options on a slow exhale. Her eyes blink, then find mine. I do all I can to implore her to open up to me. Saying as much as I can without words.

"You know that guy we ran into at the biergarten?"

"In Solvang? Wearing all those muscles? Yeah, I remember," I bristle.

"We dated before I moved to LA."

"My Spidey senses were tingling."

"He broke up with me."

"His loss," I say before Raven cuts me off.

"Please, Liam. Let me get all this out. Ok?"

"Right. Yeah. Of course. Go on. I'm listening."

"I got pregnant when I was seventeen."

"Wow," I softly exclaim.

Raven silences me with a look. "I got pregnant at seventeen," she repeats, almost like she needed to say it again to believe it herself. "And I don't know…Everything about it seemed inevitable. I grew up around so much of that. Hell, my own mother was a teen mom. I had it in my head that was the way my life was meant to be. Fated. And it wasn't even that I totally hated the prospect. Aspects of that life seemed very nice to me.

"There was pressure from both sets of parents, but Brett didn't want to get married. Said he would look after me and the baby. His parents had some money, more than my family anyway, and they were going to help out. I could see the next thirty years of my life, traveling ceaselessly down an empty one-way street. Young mama in a small town. It seemed like the only possible story."

Raven pauses as she adjusts on the couch. "Then a month later, I miscarried. And it was like a switch went off. All of a sudden, these same people who were upset I was pregnant in the first place—even if they didn't say it outright, I knew—now they were devastated at the loss I caused them. Me. As if the physical pain wasn't excruciating enough. And it was. Plenty painful. Brett blamed me. His parents blamed me. Even my mother said that baby was the best chance I had."

Raven shakes slightly, her eyes boring into her now neglected wine glass. As if the rest of the story will materialize somehow from the liquid within. I don't know what to say yet, so I don't say anything. Just listen and wait.

Eventually, she goes on. "'The best chance I had.' I'll never forget the way she looked when she said that to me. The eyes of the dreamless." Raven's deep browns shone slightly at the memory. "I never gave voice to my dreams. Never felt I'd been given permission. But at that exact moment, I knew. I had to believe in myself. No one else was going to."

Another pause that feels too sacred for my intervention. I simply stare at the contours of her face, a smoothness that belies such a jagged hurt. Her fair white skin a sharp contrast to this dark part of her past. She fills the void again. "I left the next week. Packed one suitcase, hopped on the bus, and came to LA. Hadn't talked to Brett since then. Barely spoken with my mother. Haven't looked back."

In the ensuing silence, we both take a deep breath. I search my mind for the right words. All my mouth manages is, "That must have been devastating for you. Hell, must still be painful."

"It does fucking suck." she confesses bluntly.

"I can only imagine. I'm so sorry you had to give up so much to be able to chase your dreams. I wish I could devour your pain."

"Well, now you know. No more secrets," she says with a hint of energy returning to her words. Her lips lift. A painted smile. A mask of her own.

I find my voice. "Hey, Blackbird," I rasp, seeking her eyes. "I believe in you."

I lean across the edge of the table to take her hand, allowing the motion to pull me off the chair and onto the couch next to her. I slide my arm around her shoulders and pull her into me. Her head resting where my chest meets my shoulder, her arm serpentines around my inner thigh. Holding her. Wishing for forever in this moment.

Then, finally, in a moment of shared calm I ask, "Do you think I could have a glass of wine now?"

CHAPTER THIRTY-SIX

We spend the rest of the evening talking. And while my physical desire for Raven has never burned so brightly, this feels right. The two of us, drinking a little, sharing a lot, connecting in this quiet space, alone. It feels intimate. Healing.

Bottle of pinot grigio emptied and one frozen pizza consumed, Raven and I lounge comfortably on the couch together. We dip our toes into my real past, my life with Ryan growing up in Cincy. Not that I have any reservations about revealing all of this to Raven, but the pain still seems a little raw, so we take it slow.

As we both begin to doze off on the couch, succumbing to the emotional exhaustion of the last few days, there is still part of this night that feels unsettled. A desire left unfulfilled. I ask Raven to ensure she feels the same pull. "Can I kiss you now, Rave?"

She doesn't answer. Not with words, anyway. Instead, she answers by closing the distance between us on the couch and running her long nails up my taut back. My skin pebbles at the combination of her intense stare and seductive touch. Her hands clasp firmly behind my neck as she pulls me into her, breaking eye contact only when our lips first touch. The smell of oranges invades my senses as her soft lips and devilish tongue take me in. Our eyes close as we surrender to each other, to this moment. My hands instinctively reach around her, drawing her as close to me as physics will allow.

After a few blissful moments entwined with Raven, I lean back on the couch and pull her into my chest. She melts against me, her inky tendrils dancing along my neck and shoulder, her full breasts pressed to my ribs. An unbound duality, my body both tingles with passion and calms at her nearness. My cock impossibly hard; my heart serenely soft. And it is like this—swept up in a tornado of feelings, while simultaneously sheltered from the storm by those very same feelings—that Raven and I fall asleep together on her couch, blissfully together.

At some point in the middle of the night, we manage to take ourselves to her bed which is where we find ourselves now as the morning sun filters soft light into her bedroom. Raven's relaxed, even breathing tells me she's still sleeping. I spend several minutes enjoying this quiet peace, though I must admit, my cock is as hard this morning as it was when we fell asleep last night. It has been so long since I've been with this siren, my need for her so great that it seems quite possible that I've been hard this entire time.

Determined to build us back as strong as ever, I resign myself to sneaking out so Raven can take this at her own pace, entirely on her own terms. I tiptoe into the bathroom to freshen up, then return to her room briefly to lay one chaste kiss on her forehead before leaving.

My Blackbird coos softly, her throaty rumble enough to rattle my bones. "Are you leaving?"

"I didn't want to overdo it too soon. I know this will take time."

One lithe arm emerges from underneath the comforter as Raven takes a fistful of my shirt. "It will take even more time if you leave this house right now before you show me just how much you've missed me."

"In that case—" I growl next to her ear before taking the lobe into my mouth and sucking greedily. I slide myself fully onto the bed, then straddle her. My body atop her bedspread, hers tauntingly underneath, the single layer of fabric feels like an ocean of distance. I continue peppering her face and throat with kisses, then raise up on my knees to take her in.

Holding eye contact with her, I bring my right hand along the outside of her face, admiring her delicate beauty as I run my fingers to her collarbone, then roll off her body grabbing the sheet as I go, unwrapping this exquisite present.

Raven rises slightly to remove the tank she slept in, her marvelous tits now on full display, and I undo the button on my jeans to relieve some of the pressure on my throbbing cock.

I pull my shirt over my head, then return all my attention to Raven.

"I'll start at the top and work my way down. All I need from you is to relax," I say with a devilish smirk.

Her eyes dance with recognition. "Why does that sound so familiar?"

"That's what you told me the first time we met."

"Before taking your measurements."

"Exactly. And I've wanted to do this ever since."

The time for words ends, and the time for action begins. And now that I am here, I plan to take my time. I am in no rush to rediscover every delicious inch of her body.

I encage her beneath me, allowing my body weight to gently press against her. Raven's arms go around my shoulders, inviting me closer. Propped on one elbow, I use my right hand to caress her cheek, then firmly grasp the back of her neck. A tsunami of emotions passes between us as our eyes lock. A thousand unsaid apologies and adorations pour from me as I inch closer to her, and our lips collide. One luxurious swipe of my tongue against hers and I'm lost. Raven deepens our kiss, and my body ignites. Need courses through me until I have no choice but to break the kiss, so I can taste more of her.

"I only ever want to worship you," I murmur against the soft skin under her jaw as I trail wet kisses down her throat.

My fingertips trace a line from her collarbone to her breast. My thumb brushes over her pebbled nipple before I eagerly draw it into my mouth, swirling my tongue around the bud. I devour her flesh, sucking, squeezing, and nibbling in a dizzying rhythm. I drown in her soft cleavage and damn sure ain't looking for a life preserver.

Raven's low moans turn feral as the pressure of my hands and teeth mount, but the relentless grinding of her hips against my clothed cock spurs me on. Reluctantly but speedily, I pull myself off the bed to rid myself of these cumbersome jeans. Raven's morning eyes take in all of me and a mischievous glint sparks behind them. Before I can return to the bed, Raven purrs, "Mr. O'Connell, you certainly seem to be *fully* awake this morning."

Her eyes are shamelessly glued to my rock-hard length as I smirk. "You do this to me, Blackbird. Only you. Always you."

"Yeah?"

"Fuck yeah."

"And how do I know you're telling the truth now, WilLiam?"

"I swear to you, Raven. A dishonest word won't pass from these lips ev—"

She cuts me off with a sadistic sneer, "Stroke yourself."

"What?"

"Stroke your long dick while I consider whether I'm truly ready to forgive you."

Her eyes travel down my naked frame as my hand travels to the root of my cock. Slowly, I stroke while Raven licks her lips. She kicks the remaining scraps of the sheet from her feet, then slides her panties down her magnificent legs, dangling the lace on her toe before dropping it seductively on the floor.

Throughout that tantalizing display, her almond eyes never break contact with the show I'm putting on for her. Eventually, with a playful smirk, she drags her eyes up my body to lock with mine as her slender hand covers her exposed mound, slowly beginning to circle her clit.

Standing there in front of my girl, words that are just as raw and vulnerable as my fully-exposed form pour from me. "I never meant to hurt you, Rave. I should never have let that get so out of hand."

She doesn't speak, though her silence doesn't seem to hold any malice. At least I hope it doesn't. Our breathing and the soft friction of my fist and her fingers are the only sounds in the room. Tension mixes with carnality as Raven toys with me.

I steal a glance down at her hand which hides a deliciously glistening surprise. "Do I have to beg, Rave?"

"Getting on your knees does sound like a good place to start, Irish." She arches one eyebrow as she needles the nickname into me. Like a good boy, I do as I'm told. I descend to my knees on the side of the bed as Raven swivels around to place her feet on the side of the bed frame, her perfect pussy perched just off the edge of the mattress. Raven makes an inverted V with her two fingers peeking her throbbing clit between them. "Apologize," she implores, and there isn't even a full breath before my head is buried firmly between her thighs. My tongue tickles the space between her fingers, sending a moan and shiver through her body. My hands immediately grab the insides of her creamy thighs and I firmly spread her open for me. I pull my tongue off her clit, long enough to give her one long laving from the bottom to the top. When my head peeks up between her thighs, I see her staring down at me.

With imploring eyes, I growl the word "forgive" into her core with a firm lick. She gasps lightly as I take a breath and return to her center. "Me," I plead again, sending vibrations through her. "Blackbird," I punctuate my plea with another desperate swipe at her delicious cunt.

Then again. And again. Licking her like the first popsicle of the hottest fucking summer. After several needy swipes, I press my mouth hungrily over her cunt.

"Please," the tortured word pulls from me, as my fool tongue puts itself to the best work it can at that point, alternately diving inside her then kissing her clit. My pacing is steady, though my need for her release is frantic. Forgoing any more language, I pour my apology into a greedy barrage of licks, taking command of her cunt with a firm squeeze of my hands to her thighs, allowing Raven to succumb to the pleasure.

I can feel the telltale shake of her thighs as I grip, and I know that she's close. I release my hold and relinquish some of that control, but immediately bring my hands around to cup her ass and pull her body decadently closer to my eager face. One thrust of her hips and she comes.

Violently.

Furiously.

Passionately.

As her quivering subsides, I pepper kisses between her thighs which she repeatedly squirms away from, still too sensitive for my stimulation which only makes me want to eat her more. Her giggles and moans fill the air as I reach for a condom on the nightstand, then come up to my full height. Before I sheath myself, I grip my engorged cock and stroke it twice as I center myself above Raven's soaked pussy, still tauntingly open for me off the side of the bed. I lay the weight of my cock over her opening and grind slowly, slicking my shaft with her wetness, but the stimulation must still be too much too soon because before I know it, Raven spins a hundred and eighty degrees on the mattress, her dark hair now pouring off the side, her mouth now poised below my dick.

"Can I take this to mean you appreciated that apology?" I ask, low in my throat.

Her eyes lock with mine and Raven assumes control, even in this most vulnerable position. "Fuck my face, Liam," she demands, ignoring my question, as she opens her mouth, coaxing me forward.

I watch the head disappear between her suctioning cheeks, as I rock into her ever-so-slowly. I can feel her relax on a devilish moan as she takes me down further. "Fuck," I growl, "watching my cock fill your throat is the sexiest fucking thing I've ever seen."

I toss the still-wrapped condom onto the bed because the urge to use both hands on her sinful body is too much to resist. I take her tits firmly in my hands, then slowly and repeatedly fill her face with my dick, unsure what I did to deserve this woman. After a few moments, she taps my ass with her hand and I know immediately to pull out of her. Raven gasps and flips herself over and up onto all fours, her eyes watering, one decadent trail of saliva painting the side of her chin.

"You're the most incredible creature," I praise, then grab her jaw and kiss her. The taste of me on her tongue mixes with the taste of her on mine in the most intoxicating elixir of sensuality. I push in toward her, forcing her body back onto the bed, my hand bringing her head down on the pillows as her body turns and her legs spread for me. I grab the condom off of the duvet, then climb onto the bed on my hands and knees. The second our bodies are in close enough proximity to each other, my dick finds its way to her core in one smooth stroke. With my pelvis pressed firmly against her clit, we grind in to each other. My cock fills her fully, yet somehow we both want more. I thrust a little further as I bring one hand down to her ass to guide her hips up just slightly. The fraction of an inch is all she needs, and on a moan that is mostly pleasure with a hint of delicious pain, my Blackbird soars.

Her second orgasm comes in waves and I do everything I can to hold on. When Raven's breathing begins to even out and her eyes open again, I adjust my pace to fuck her in smooth strokes- sliding the head of my dick all the way to the entrance of her slick folds and then pushing inch after inch slowly back into her.

I'm not sure if we keep this rhythm for several seconds, minutes, or even hours, but my brain can only register that I could stay like this forever. It would seem Raven has different ideas though, because that naughty gleam returns to her eyes, and in one powerful motion, she bucks her hips and reverses our positions on the bed without our bodies ever coming apart. I'm now pressed squarely into the mattress, Raven straddling me like a deadly predator seconds before devouring their prey. A smile paints her face as she presses her hands into my chest, a predator indeed.

I thrust up off the bed once, spearing her with my length and Raven rakes her nails down my chest on a gasp. Once. Hard.

"That fucking hurt," I say in shock, glancing at the red lines forming instantly on my chest.

"Good," she growls low in her throat- a puma's purr- then brings her mouth to mine and kisses me. Once. Even harder.

Fully in control, Raven rocks and rides atop me and I willingly relent. I watch as her tits bounce and her hips sway. Raven owns my body and my mind as she pumps, pounds, and pounces on me. When her hand reaches behind her ass to massage my balls, I groan involuntarily. All these sensations—the warm gliding of her cunt, the steely grip of her hands on my quads, the slight burn on my chest—overwhelm and I warn, "I'm gonna come."

Raven releases my thighs, pressing her pillowy tits against my chest and whispers into my ear, "You fucking better."

So I do. My legs tense, my ass clenches, and jolt after jolt of ecstasy overtakes me. The strength of my thrusts and the power of our connection sends Raven over one more time too, and we finish together. Blissfully. After several moments, our cheeks still pressed together, Raven purrs again, "Apology accepted."

"Yeah?" I growl back excitedly.

"For now," she coos, then bites the lobe of my ear. A little harder than playful. She giggles maniacally, then presses her head into my chest as we close our eyes for a few minutes of postcoital bliss.

Sweaty and sated, Raven and I lie in a tangled heap in her bed. The labor of our breathing and the heady aroma in the air both testaments to the power of our passion. I gently slide her off me so I can head to the bathroom to clean up. I return with a warm washcloth to clean her off as well, then we return to the simple pleasure of lying next to each other.

After some time, Raven's words cut through my euphoric daze. "Can I ask you something?"

"Yeah. Anything." I turn my head to give her more of my focus.

"Before you left for Montana, when you dropped me off, had you meant to tell me?"

"Yes."

"But instead, you..." She leaves my declaration of love left unsaid, hanging between us.

"Yes. And I meant it. I do mean it." I prop up on my elbow to look directly into her eyes. "I hope you'll give me a million more opportunities to prove it to you."

She eyes me thoughtfully before a warmth lights her chestnut eyes. "Well, this was a good start."

"The sex? I agree. That we should definitely do again."

"All of it, you ass," she reproaches playfully. "The whole night."

"And this morning," I add on.

"You know what would make it perfect?"

"What's that?"

"Breakfast tacos."

"Absolutely," I agree, folding her in my arms. It's always a yes to breakfast tacos.

CHAPTER THIRTY-SEVEN

Half an hour later, Raven and I sit in a wood plank booth with two metal trays of egg and cheese goodness wrapped in the best flour tortillas Los Angeles has to offer. We toast to her successful first live event—and a whole lot more—with coffee in our Home State embossed ceramic camping mugs.

"To the future," Raven offers.

"To right fucking now." I declare.

We drink and dive in to our *neches* and *comal* tacos. After a few bites, Raven speaks.

"Liam, seriously. That was a really thoughtful thing you did. Having Abigail come."

"I had nothing to do with that," I insist. "All I did was ask her."

"Well it took something special to do that just for me. It was—"

"Nothing." I cut her off. "I believe in you. And look, I'm sorry if this isn't fair of me to say or whatever, but I fucking love you. And I'm proud of you. Proud of the woman I love. And honestly, truly. I did that because you deserve it. Not because I thought I deserved you. You fucking shine and the world needs your light. That's it."

Raven responds emphatically. "I love you too, William O'Connell."

I stop short. "What did you say?"

"You heard me."

"Really? You mean it?"

"Yeah, I mean it. I love you." Her tone vibrates with excitement, but also with ease. There's an instant comfort in it.

Something comes over me and I cannot help myself. I jump to my feet and shout. Well, it's more like a holler.

"Whooooo!"

All eyes in the restaurant turn our way, but I do not care. In fact, I welcome the audience. "You hear that, everyone? She loves me too. She said it. She meant it. This is happening!"

Raven's pale cheeks flush as does the delectable expanse of skin I can see above her chest. She shushes me and insists I sit down which I do, using my outburst as an excuse to move on to her side of the booth.

And although it's early and we've been eating tacos and drinking coffee, I do not care. I still punctuate this moment with a kiss. Not just *a* kiss, the best kiss of my life. A moment unchained from anxiety, steeped in passion, and filled with love. Raven and I drown out the sea of disinterested diners around us and live in this blissful moment alone, together.

Our connection breaks when the joy becomes almost too much to bear. We look at each other and giggle. Dizzy from happiness, a conversation I overheard at Lexi's party comes rushing into my mind and I share these uncensored thoughts with Raven.

"Rave, the other day at Lexi's party, I overheard my niece and her mom talking. And it got me thinking."

"Okay," she drawls slowly, responding to my serious shift in tone.

"It's all good," I try to assure her. "Just this moment I wanted to tell you about because it got me thinking about you, about us. Anyway," I continue before I lose my head of steam. "Lexi asked Hazel when cake was happening, and her mom said five minutes. In response, Lexi, who's still learning how to tell time, asked if that was long or short. And instantly I thought, five minutes. That's short. Not that long at all."

"Sure," Raven inserts taking a sip from her coffee mug.

"Right? But then Hazel went on this riff about how time is relative, and that context matters and that the amount of time isn't necessarily as important as what that time is meant to fill. And I instantly thought of you. Because since I met you, time doesn't mean what it used to."

"What do you mean?"

"When I look at you, a second could be a lifetime. That's how richly I *feel* being with you. But when I spend the day with you, it passes like the blink of an eye. That's how joyously I experience the world with you. I'm so fucking into you that time has lost its inherent meaning to me and all I know is that I want to spend more of it with you."

I exhale after finishing that declaration and then look for my neglected taco on the table. Before I can reach for it, Raven places her hand on my stubbled cheek and crashes her crimson lips on mine.

"That was fucking hot, Irish," she whispers into my lips, and her use of her old nickname for me feels like a peace offering, an earnest attempt to help us both move forward without losing the completeness of our story. It's music to my ears.

But my ecstasy is short-lived, as Raven then pulls further away to say, "I'm really bummed I missed that party. Was looking forward to it for quite a while."

"Ugh. Me too," I grunt shamefully. "I'm so sorry about that. It fucking gutted me. I hope you know that, and family is a big deal to me, and I cannot wait for you to spend more time with Ryan and the girls."

"I know, Liam. We'll get there."

"Actually," I say as a thought occurs to me in real-time. "Devontay and I bought Lexi and her parents a night at Medieval Times as her birthday present. Would you do me the distinct pleasure of coming with me as my royal date?" I ask, slipping into a haughty British accent to formalize the occasion.

Raven's smile sets my entire being on fire. "Medieval Times fucking rocks!"

I laugh as she continues, matching my pompous accent as she declares, "I would love to, my liege. I hope my presence brings great honor to the kingdom."

INTERLUDE #9

Out out, damn spots.

HEY THERE, MY STITCHES. ON THIS EDITION OF *RAGS TO RAVEN*, WE'RE going to be tackling the scourge of the fashion world. And no, it's not capris. I'm talking about stains. Chocolate and red wine are too delicious to forgo, but they can be an outfit killer. And let's face it. Awful things can happen to even the best of your looks. So, what to do when something that feels so right when you put it on looks so wrong when you see it in the mirror? Sometimes an outfit needs a little faith and a lot of TLC to come back even better than ever. Love and a few household items, anyway.

So here are the key ingredients you need to have on hand to ensure that no blemishes stop you from rocking any of your favorite looks: dish soap, vinegar, baking soda, a toothbrush, and some alcohol.

Yes, occasionally rubbing alcohol can help get some tough oil stains out of cotton, but in other situations, a nice rosé will help you get through a stain removal session, too. So always be prepared.

And remember, if something awful happens to something you love, don't fret. Fix it. If you love a piece in your wardrobe, then don't throw it away. See if you can't knock out those stains and bring that piece back even better than before. Because now that item has a story! And not only have you salvaged something beautiful, you've given yourself a welcome reminder too. That you care enough about something to nurture it and make it shine again.

CHAPTER THIRTY-EIGHT

As the sun sets in Buena Park, my family, friends, and I set our sights on a Medieval castle, complete with a moat, bridge, and imposing giant red door. Lexi leads the charge as we storm past the battlements seeking entertainment. Von takes Lexi to the check-in desk where we are issued crowns and ushered to our seats. From the moment we cross through that imposing scarlet entrance, the world transports us back to a land over a thousand years ago. Lexi seems instantly invested in the pageantry which makes it so much more fun for the five adults who have joined her to get involved in the action.

Holding Raven's hand, a sensation I did not realize I would love so much, we find our row in the green knight's section, and we help each other don our paper crowns. Von sits to the right of Raven who is next to me with Lexi on my left and her parents bookend our group. Once seated, we all raise a glass of our beverages of choice and toast the lady of the evening, the Fair Maiden Lexi. Though I must admit, sitting sandwiched between the woman I love and the family I adore, I cannot help but feel a special energy tonight.

I smile over at Von, silently relishing the joy of the family one makes in life. A bond formed purely out of love, never out of obligation. My eyes then travel to Raven and pinpricks of passion shoot down my arms and legs as I think about the bond forging itself between the two of us. I take her hand in mine and plant a soft, meaningful kiss near her ear, then whisper, "I'm so fucking happy that you're here tonight."

She moans slightly and returns my heated gaze, whispering in a lust-tinged voice, "Me too. Now switch seats with me so I can sit next to the birthday princess."

I laugh, rising and bowing to both Lexi and Rave as I sidle over and plop down next to Devontay. He and I clink glasses as the lights fade to half and the show begins.

"Kings, Queens, and Jesters. Squires, Bards, and Peasants. Tonight, we feast. Tonight, we fight. Tonight, we determine who is the Champion of the Realm. Welcome to Medieval Times," the town crier booms throughout the arena to thunderous applause. Our group joins in the revelry as the sandy floor of the indoor oval shakes with galloping steeds parading their knights around the space.

Lexi 'oohs' when the horses appear, the draped knights filling the space.

"There he is," Lexi shouts. "That's our green knight on the pretty white horse. He definitely looks the fiercest. We've got this in the bag."

For the next couple of hours, we immerse ourselves in this fantasy world, cheering at the well-choreographed fight sequences and marveling at the impressive equestrian skills. The latter is clearly the part of the show that has most of Lexi and Raven's attention as they spend the evening complimenting the horses and discussing the costumes. The storytelling elements excite Lexi's fertile imagination, though she does complain at one point that "The show should definitely have some dragons."

We all roundly agree, Raven going so far as to say she'll send sketches to the company's customer service inbox.

At this Ryan chimes in, yelling slightly to be heard over the roar of the crowd. "I doubt that will work, Raven. They didn't have email in Medieval England."

"Is this meant to be England?" Hazel jumps in on the joke. "Is this how they think the British sound?"

Lexi bristles playfully at her parents. "It's called suspension of disbelief, Mom. Give it a try. If you need help, I'm sure Uncle Liam can help you out."

There's light laughter from the group at my expense, though I admit to being slightly thrown off hearing my niece call me Liam. "Lexi," I cut in. "You can always call me Uncle Will."

"Oh, I don't mind, Uncle Liam," she repeats the name effortlessly. "That's what Raven calls you. And I will call you whatever she wants as long as she sticks around. So don't mess this up. Ok, Uncle Liam?" She smirks as her eyes twinkle.

"I don't intend to, Lexi Sprout. I really don't." That last sentence I pitch toward Raven, taking hold of her soft hand as we make eye contact. I start leaning toward my Blackbird to give her another chaste kiss because I basically don't want to ever stop kissing her, but our attention shoots to the stage at the loud clang of steel on steel. Our very own Green Knight finds himself battling for the evening's biggest prize against the Red and Yellow Knight.

"Come on, Greenie. Slit his traitorous throat," Lexi yells menacingly.

Devontay laughs and leans toward me. "She might still have been a little young for this birthday present, buddy."

I look over to see Hazel and Ryan laughing. As long as the parents don't scowl, we are in the clear. "I think we did good, Von. Another epic birthday experience in the books."

"Another chapter written," he says proudly. And I wholeheartedly agree with a silent fist bump.

Then my attention turns to the stunningly beautiful Blackbird that flew into my life a short time ago and stole my heart. His comment has me thinking about my next chapter. The one I will get to write with Raven. The songs we have yet to sing, the stories we have yet to write. My heart swells at the soaring possibility of it all. And as I sit in this makeshift castle in Anaheim, surrounded by those dearest to me, I take in the wildly talented Queen beside me, thinking to myself: that is a book I cannot wait to read. One I know will end with a happily ever after.

EPILOGUE

Six Months Later

"For a girl who never went to prom, two limos in one month feels like the best revenge," my sexy vixen says from the plush leather seat next to me in the back of our stretch Escalade.

I lean over and plant a firm kiss on her ruby-red lips, sliding my tongue into her mouth in one needy stroke. She tastes like desire and the lingering sweetness of Prosecco. My cock swells instantly against the thin fabric of my black tux pants.

Last week, we took a different limousine to the Emmy Awards where somehow, I was not only nominated, but managed to win for Best Guest Star in a TV Series. Tonight, we are heading to the Fox Theatre in Westwood for the premiere of *Nowhere to Hide*.

As our lips part, I tell Rave, "I will dress you up and take you out dancing any time. Hell, I'll even throw in a round of awkward two-minute sex in a budget hotel if you want."

She purrs an intoxicating laugh. "Sounds like I didn't miss much."

"Safe to say prom is overrated."

Something that is definitely not overrated, however: these past few months with Raven. They have been nothing short of incredible. From date nights and lounging on the couch during the week to epic weekend adventures, we love living life together. And in fact, began actually living together recently. I traded the dunes for Dodger Stadium and moved in with her. Her roommate Willow has embarked on a nine-month adventure with a production company to shoot a documentary about nomadic living, so the place is ours until then.

And then? We'll figure that next step out. Raven's designs sell out faster than she can make them. She now also has a *Rags to Raven* retail space in about a dozen boutiques in LA. Meanwhile, we leave next month to shoot a film together.

In a poetic twist of fate, I have been cast as an Irishman infiltrating the Dublin underground to avenge my murdered father. With the director's blessing, Raven will be working wardrobe and we will spend a month together on the banks of the River Liffey.

Right now though, my Blackbird transfixes me to the present as she notices the bulge in my pants, then trails her sultry brown eyes up to meet mine.

"Well, hello there, Mr. Emmy Winner. Mind if I take a peek at your golden statue?" She tiptoes her fingers across the space between us, then up the ridge of my thigh until she has taken firm hold of me. My guttural moan she takes rightly as consent, and with her eyes locked firmly on mine, she expertly unclasps my dress pants and pulls out my aching length.

She massages me slowly as I drink her in, a skin-tight scarlet dress hugging her along each of her decadent curves. "Rave, you are fucking magic," I rasp, leaning in to take her mouth, but she leans back, a devilish grin on her face.

"If you think I'm magic, wait until you see the tricks I built into this dress," she coos, because of course, Raven designed and built her own dress for the premiere.

I quickly double-check that the privacy partition is raised as Raven leaves her seat, floats to her knees between my legs, and buries my cock down her throat in one effortless motion. "Fuuuuuuuuuuck," I grunt as she slowly teases her tongue back up the length of my shaft. On a soft popping sound, she draws her body up my thighs, her breasts teasing my dick as she continues her ascent. Then she guides my hand along her hip and down to the hem of her skin-tight dress.

"Feel that?" she asks, placing my hand on the clasp of a tiny zipper.

I grunt my acknowledgment.

"Pull it," she demands as I slowly slide the zipper up her thigh, allowing her legs to part enough for her to straddle me.

"I've been staring at you in that dress for an hour and I had no idea there was a zipper on the side."

"I'm very good at what I do," Rave moans, her hips swaying slowly over my clenched abs.

"Yes, you are."

The fact that my Blackbird does not have any underwear on becomes abundantly clear the next moment when I can feel her wet entrance kiss the top of my crown. She holds herself above me momentarily, her hand gripped firmly around the base of my cock. In the months we've been together, we have never gone bare. Raven seems poised to change that. She whispers to me, "I'm on the pill."

My response comes out unbidden, but no less honest for all that. "It would be okay with me if you weren't."

Raven grins slyly. "Take it easy there, slugger. We're in the back of a limo."

"Right," I groan, sliding my hands from the tops of her thighs to grab her round ass cheeks greedily. "What do you want me to do?"

She purrs against my ear, licking and biting along the outside. "Right now, I want you to shut up and let me ride your dick."

I am only too happy to oblige as Raven slowly sinks down, taking her fill. And holy shit, she may be my Blackbird, but right now she has me flying, taking me away as the silky feel of our unhindered connection sends me into orbit. It takes only a few short moments—moments that feel like blissful hours because time with Raven plays by its own rules—to climax together. The euphoric feel of our wholly connected bodies is too much for either of us to hold out long.

She slides off me and melts back into her seat. In a haze, I reach for a towel off the limo's wet bar to clean us both up. Raven resets the phantom zipper on the side of her dress just as the vehicle slows and the soft flashes and din of the paparazzi make their way through the tinted windows.

"You are..." The sentence lingers unfinished because Raven is everything to me and no one particular word seems appropriate.

"I know," she retorts playfully as we lean in for one more kiss. Our eyes lock, sharing an unspoken connection. We take a deep breath.

Then we open the door, step out of the limo, and into the future. Hand in hand.

THE END.

Author. Advocate. Ally.

One of the romance genre's most prolific and beloved voice actors, Joe Arden, is a proud advocate for equality, consent, and respect.

His deeply emotional performances and character connectivity have made him a fan favorite, bringing hundreds of memorable characters to life over the years. "Arden's smoky baritone, passionate and believable, packs a wallop in the sultry department," exclaims AudioFile Magazine.

His solo writing debut, "The Chameleon Effect," was shortlisted by Audible's Editorial Staff as "one of the Best Audiobooks of 2022," earned an Earphones Award, and was voted one of the "Top 100 Romance Audios of All Time." Joe has been featured in Men's Health magazine and honored with numerous industry awards.

He is the CEO of Blue Nose Audio, a boutique company focused on helping independent authors turn their written works into dynamic and marketable audiobook experiences.

When he isn't in the studio, writing his next chapter, or connecting with his fans and hearing their stories, Joe enjoys hiking, traveling, and investing his time and heart in supporting Pitbull foster and rescue efforts.

And if you want exclusive, behind-the-scenes access to all the content Joe is creating, join him and his army of self-love warriors on Patreon today.

Joe Arden's Audio Attic.
patreon.com/JoeArden

www.TheRealJoeArden.com

SOCIALS

facebook.com/TheRealJoeArden

instagram.com/TheRealJoeArden

TikTok.com/@therealjoearden

www.bookbub.com/authors/joe-arden

www.goodreads.com/author/show/20682028.Joe_Arden

ACKNOWLEDGEMENTS

To the women of Romancelandia: the authors, the narrators, the fans.

Thank you for allowing me to play in your castle.

I am a proud jester in a court of Queens, but you all make me feel like a King.

To CL—Your belief in me is a coat of armor.

To D & T—you are two good friends I turned into one great character.

To Maxine Mitchell—you are a phenomenal talent and I love collaborating with you. Thanks for your help on this one.

To Brittney and Victoria—your organization fuels my ambition.

To Riley Edwards—your constant word count check-ins and text messages were a huge pain in the ass. I am grateful for every single one of them.

To Kate Stewart—your generosity of time and resources will never be forgotten. I would say the first round is on me, but it doesn't matter who gets the first round, because it damn sure won't be the only round.

To Rebecca Hodgkins—thanks for helping make this a much better book.

To Autumn Gantz—thanks for helping me find an audience.

To the members of The Audio Attic—We keep building this castle in the clouds. It's so pretty up here with you all.

And finally, to my Dad—thanks for helping me write all those essays in high school. Was that cheating? Technically, yes, I believe it was. But hey, we had a great time together and I learned a lot.

www.ingramcontent.com/pod-product-compliance
Lightning Source LLC
Chambersburg PA
CBHW070631310726
48982CB00001B/246

* 9 7 9 8 9 9 1 5 9 2 2 4 6 *